NICOLA BERRY

FOR GEORGE
—LM

PENGUIN WORKSHOP
Penguin Young Readers Group
An Imprint of Penguin Random House LLC

Text copyright © 2009 by Liane Moriarty.
Cover illustration copyright © 2018 by Rebecca Mock.
All rights reserved. First published in 2009 as *Nicola Berry:
Earthling Ambassador: The Shobble Secret* by Grosset & Dunlap.
This edition published in 2018 by Penguin Workshop,
an imprint of Penguin Random House LLC,
345 Hudson Street, New York, New York 10014.
PENGUIN and PENGUIN WORKSHOP are trademarks of
Penguin Books Ltd, and the W colophon is a trademark of
Penguin Random House LLC. Printed in the USA.

Cover illustration by Rebecca Mock
Design by Sara Corbett
The text in this book is set in Surveyor.

The Library of Congress has cataloged the Grosset & Dunlap
edition under the following Control Number: 2008027520

ISBN 9781524788094   10 9 8 7 6 5 4 3 2 1

LIANE MORIARTY

NICOLA BERRY

AND THE SHOCKING TROUBLE ON THE PLANET OF SHOBBLE

PENGUIN WORKSHOP ★ AN IMPRINT OF PENGUIN RANDOM HOUSE

PROLOGUE

TWO GIRLS AND A BOY STOOD KNEE-DEEP IN SNOW on the side of a mountain. A thousand dazzling rainbows soared above them. Beneath them a frozen sea shimmered like a giant sapphire.

The shorter of the girls had curly red-gold hair that blew in a halo around her head and dimples that dented her cheeks.

She was in an extremely bad mood.

"Are you sure it's true?" she snapped.

"No. I made the whole thing up just to ruin your day." The boy sighed. He was her younger brother, which explains a lot.

The other girl, who had dark brown frizzy hair and a serious pale face, didn't say anything. She was thinking, pressing her finger hard against her bottom lip.

The girl with the red-gold hair blew her nose noisily. She said, "I just never thought things would go this far. It's frightening."

"Yes," admitted the boy. "But we'll fight!"

"Of course we'll fight! What is this evil Earthling's name?"

The boy pulled out a sheet of paper from his back pocket and examined it.

"Nicola," he answered. "Nicola Berry."

**ICOLA BERRY HAD A PROBLEM.**

She needed to make a long-distance phone call.

An *extremely* long-distance phone call.

She needed to call someone who lived on another planet.

Unfortunately, whenever Nicola's mother checked the phone bill lately, she made a sound like she had a fish bone stuck in her throat. If an intergalactic phone call appeared on the bill she might stop breathing altogether.

Nicola pondered her problem while she cut up a banana to put on top of her breakfast cereal. The house was still and silent. A shaft of summer sunlight was creeping its way across the kitchen floor. It was early Saturday morning and her brother and parents were still sound asleep. They wouldn't be up for hours, when they would appear rubbing their eyes and saying things like, "You're up already? *Why?*"

While Nicola ate her cereal at the kitchen table, she frowned as she studied the newspaper clipping her dad had pinned to the notice board. The headline read:

NICOLA AND HER FRIENDS SAVE THE WORLD!

She still got the strangest feeling from seeing her name in a newspaper. Nicola read the first paragraph of the article again.

Last week, Nicola Berry and a group of young friends she refers to as the "Space Brigade" undertook a daring intergalactic mission to kill an unspeakably evil alien princess called Princess Petronella, who had been left in charge of the planet of Globagaskar while her parents were on vacation. The spoiled young princess came up with a despicable plan to destroy Earth. Fortunately, Nicola and her young friends found out about the plan. They traveled to Globagaskar by spaceship and kidnapped the princess from her palace bedroom . . . The princess is dead and Earth has been saved, thanks to the heroic efforts of the Space Brigade.

The newspaper reporter had got it wrong. Nicola and the Space Brigade had kidnapped the princess and convinced her not to destroy Earth, but they certainly hadn't killed her! She was very much alive and kicking.

Actually, she was kicking all day long, according to her latest Glext (intergalactic e-mail—sent from the superadvanced computer in the Globagaskar Palace all the way through outer space and cyberspace to the Berry family's battered old computer in their living room). The princess had Glexted to say that her new hobby was kick-boxing and she was spending hours practicing on her poor guards.

Without a doubt, traveling to Globagaskar and kidnapping the princess had been the scariest thing Nicola had ever done. Not surprisingly, most people assumed Nicola wasn't in a hurry to head off into outer space again. "You probably want to put your feet up, eat popcorn, and watch TV for the next twenty years or so, hey, Nic?" her dad had said hopefully.

He had no idea that Nicola was actually hoping for the Space Brigade to be on its second mission very soon.

She put down her spoon and pulled out a crumpled letter from her pocket to read it for about the 1,200th time. It said:

Dear Nicola,

    I understand you're the leader of a brigade of highly trained intergalactic freedom fighters and that you recently saved a planet by the name of EARTH.

    Our small but exquisite planet is currently facing grave danger of a rather

unusual kind and we would like to engage
your services. Payment would be both
generous and delicious.

If you are available and interested
in taking on a new mission, please
don't hesitate to call this number:
90285608248450934250890518089123094380941.

We look forward with much anticipation
to hearing from you,

> COMMANDER IN CHIEF,
> PLANET OF SHOBBLE

Nicola looked longingly at the phone. If she didn't hurry
up and call him, the commander might find another brigade
of "highly trained intergalactic freedom fighters."

Of course, the truth was that the members of the Space
Brigade weren't exactly "highly trained." Nicola felt a
flutter of fear as she considered the words *grave danger*.
Imagine if something happened to one of them and it was
Nicola's fault. Everybody would hate her. She'd never be
invited to another party for the rest of her life. Why was
she even considering it? She put her hand over the letter,
ready to crumple it up, but then her eye caught the line,
"Payment would be both generous and delicious." That
sounded so tempting.

Nicola's great-grandmother was turning one hundred
years old in a few days' time and Nicola wanted to find her

the perfect present. After all, not many people had been alive for a whole century. If they were paid with something delicious, Nicola could give it to Grammy. "This is just a little something I picked up in outer space," she could say casually.

She looked down at her cereal.

What should she do?

She slapped her hand to her forehead.

"It's pretty obvious," she said out loud.

"What's obvious?" said a voice and Nicola got such a fright that she jumped back in her chair and sent her cereal bowl flying with her elbow.

HAT ARE YOU TWO DOING HERE?" ASKED Nicola.

It was as though her best friends, Katie Hobbs and Tyler Brown, had materialized out of thin air. They were standing right in front of her wearing sunglasses and caps, with beach towels draped over their shoulders. Katie had leaped forward and caught Nicola's cereal bowl just before it landed on the floor.

"We thought you might want to come to the pool with us," Katie said. She took Nicola's cereal bowl to the sink, rinsed it out, and put it in the dishwasher.

"What's that you're reading?" asked Tyler.

Nicola pushed the letter over to him. "Read it for yourself. You too, Katie."

Katie came and read over Tyler's shoulder.

Tyler finished first and looked up. His eyes shone through his glasses and his ears glowed pink.

"When are we going? Have you called the commander yet? Oh, this is just . . . this is just—I can't think of a word that's good enough!"

"Stupendous?" suggested Nicola.

"If that means really, really excellent, then yes! What do you think, Katie?"

"Ummm." Katie pulled her long brown braid from over her shoulder and chewed on the end. "I guess."

"Great!" said Tyler. "So, Nic, we've got to act fast."

"Wait a second." Nicola looked carefully at Katie. "I want to know what Katie really thinks."

Katie threw back her braid and chewed on her lip. "It's just that—"

"What?" said Tyler.

"It's just that it says *grave danger*," said Katie.

"We don't have to do it," said Nicola.

"I want to do it but I don't want to do it," said Katie. "Our first mission was the best time I've had in my whole life, but it was also the worst time. Does that make sense?"

"Yes," said Nicola.

"No," said Tyler.

"Well, anyway," continued Katie. "We don't have a choice, we've *got* to do it! They need us! All the poor people on their 'small but exquisite' planet are depending on us!"

Nicola felt guilty. All she'd thought about was how fun or scary the mission would be. She nodded gravely and frowned as if she'd been worried to death about the people of Shobble. "Yes, I know," she said. "It's a big responsibility."

"So what did you mean before when you said that it was pretty obvious?" asked Tyler.

"I realized I should just put it to the vote," said Nicola.

"Well, Sean will want to go," said Tyler confidently.

"That's true," agreed Nicola. "He'll probably complain that it doesn't sound dangerous enough."

"What about Greta?" asked Katie.

"Oh, is she still in the Brigade?" asked Tyler. "I mean, she sort of tricked us into letting her join in the first place."

"She did help with some things," said Nicola.

"She wasn't *that* bad," said Katie. "She doesn't mean to be so bossy. I kind of liked her at the end."

"Oh-kay." Nicola and Tyler gave each other doubtful looks. Sometimes Katie took being nice just a little too far.

"And then there's Shimlara," said Katie.

Shimlara was their friend from the planet of Globagaskar. Her dad was Georgio, the president of the Save the Little Earthlings Committee. Shimlara had become a member of the Space Brigade when she offered to help them kidnap Princess Petronella. Apart from the fact that Shimlara was six feet tall (the people of Globagaskar were nearly twice as tall as Earthlings) and knew how to read minds (a handy Globagaskarian skill!), she was pretty much like an ordinary Earthling girl.

"She'll want to go," said Nicola, Tyler, and Katie all at the same time.

"It looks like we already know what the vote will be," said Tyler.

Nicola picked up the letter again. "The other problem is that I need to call the commander. How much do you think it would cost to call another planet?"

At that moment Sean walked into the kitchen, yawning. "Why are you three up so *early*?" he said predictably. He opened the fridge door and stood there for a few seconds before turning around slowly. "Did you just say something about calling up another planet?"

"Yep." Nicola waved the letter at him mysteriously. "The Space Brigade might be going on another mission."

"What?" Sean slammed the fridge door shut and grabbed the letter from Nicola's hand. He read it quickly. "YES! So have you called yet? Why not? Too nervous, huh?"

"How do you think Mom and Dad would like it if I called another planet?"

"Oh. Good point."

They were all silent as they tried to think of a solution. Suddenly, the phone rang and they all jumped.

Katie, who was the nearest, picked it up.

She spoke in a bubbly, professional voice, entirely

unlike her normal voice. "Good *morning*! This is the Berry residence. How may I help you today?"

Katie learned how to answer phones from her mom, who was a receptionist at a doctor's office. If Sean had answered it, he would have said, "Yo," which always caused the person on the other end to say, "Ummm, *pardon*?"

"Nicola Berry? Yes, I'll just check if she's available. May I ask who is calling?" said Katie. Her eyes had become very wide and were rolling about wildly like a frightened horse's.

"What?" said Nicola. "Who is it?"

Katie handed the phone to Nicola and said, "It's the commander in chief of the planet of Shobble, calling for Miss Nicola Berry."

3

ELLO?" SAID NICOLA CROAKILY INTO THE PHONE. "This is Nicola speaking."

Tyler was dancing silently around the kitchen, punching the air like he'd just won a boxing match, while Katie was beaming and giving her two thumbs-up. Sean was busy writing on a piece of paper: *Don't mess up!*

Nicola tried to ignore them all and listen to the person on the other end of the phone. His voice was warm, deep, and sweet, like honey drizzled on toast.

"I do hope you don't mind me calling you. Is this perhaps an inconvenient time for a chat?"

"Oh yes, I mean no, um, this is a very convenient time," said Nicola. *Pull yourself together*, she told herself sternly. *You've got to sound like the leader of a Space Brigade, not a bumbling idiot wearing an old summer nightie with pictures of koala bears all over it.*

"My name is Enrico. Did you receive my letter, Nicola? May I call you Nicola?" asked the commander. "Please do call me Enrico."

"Yes, of course, ah, Enrico, you may call me Nicola,"

said Nicola grandly, in her poshest voice. "I did receive your letter. In fact I was just discussing it with some of my, ah, senior members of the Space Brigade."

She glanced up to see Katie, Tyler, and Sean, all stifling their laughter over her posh voice.

"My timing was fortuitous, then," said Enrico.

"Indeed," agreed Nicola, although she had no idea what *fortuitous* meant.

"And tell me, have you decided whether you would like to help us out?"

Nicola didn't hesitate. "Absolutely!" She continued on quickly, "Depending, of course, on what the mission actually involves."

Enrico said, "Of course, of course! May I suggest you drop by for dinner and a briefing? I assume you have your own transportation?"

"Yes, we do," said Nicola proudly, thinking of the mini easy-ride spaceship that Shimlara had left behind with Tyler after their last mission.

"Excellent! Shall we say six p.m.?"

Nicola was suddenly in a fluster. Six p.m.? *Today?*

"Well, it's been an absolute pleasure," said Enrico, without waiting for an answer. "I do look forward to meeting you. Oh, I'll have someone pick you up at the SpacePort, of course. Cheerio!"

The line went dead. Slowly Nicola hung up the phone. *My goodness*, she thought. *What have I done?*

"Well?" said Sean.

"We need to be on the planet of Shobble today at six p.m.," said Nicola. "For a mission briefing and dinner."

"Excellent!" said Sean.

"Did you mention we weren't exactly 'highly trained'?" asked Katie worriedly.

"What are you talking about?" said Sean. "We're the best! We kick butt!" He kicked over a chair to demonstrate.

"So when should we leave?" asked Tyler.

Everybody looked at Nicola expectantly and suddenly she remembered the huge weight of responsibility that came with being in charge. It was like walking around lugging a heavy backpack when everybody else was empty-handed.

"Okay," she said. "We'll have to pick Shimlara up from Globagaskar on the way there. I don't know how long it takes to get to Shobble and there are probably time differences, so, umm, I think we should leave Earth by no later than, ummm, ten o'clock."

"Right! Meeting at ten hundred hours." Tyler stood to attention.

Nicola said, "I don't know if it's cold or hot on Shobble so you'd better bring summer and winter clothes just in case. Oh, and pack anything else that you think might be useful."

"Like what?" asked Katie, who had actually taken out a notepad and was writing down what Nicola said. Sometimes Nicola didn't know which was worse: when the members of the Space Brigade didn't respect her, or when they *did*.

"I don't know," she admitted. "Just think creatively."

"Okay," said Katie uncertainly.

"I guess I'd better call Greta," said Nicola. "And Sean, can you send Shimlara a Glext?"

Everybody scattered. Nicola dialed Greta's number, gritting her teeth in preparation. Normally it took only about thirty seconds of conversation with Greta before Nicola found herself wanting to bang her head against the nearest wall.

"Hello?"

"Hi, Greta, it's Nicola."

"My mother says it's bad manners to call anyone this early."

Nicola turned and gently bumped her forehead against the kitchen wall.

"Sorry. It's just that the Space Brigade has another mission—"

"What? When did you hear about this? Why didn't you tell me earlier?"

"Well, umm—"

"I suppose Katie and Tyler and Sean already know about it?"

"Well, yes, sort of."

"Typical. Favoritism. A good leader shouldn't favor anyone. Anyway, I'm *very* busy today."

"Oh! Well, that's okay. I just thought I should ask—"

"But I suppose you need me. It's not like you could have managed the last mission without me. So when and where do we meet?"

"Ten o'clock at my place," said Nicola weakly. "Pack clothes for all seasons and anything that you think might be useful."

"You're not very organized—you really should have given more notice and sent out memos and a schedule. That's what I would have done. But *all right*, I'll see you then."

Nicola hung up the phone. Sean called down from the top of the stairs, "Shimlara just Glexted back! She hopes it's even *more* dangerous than last time!"

"Well, I don't!" Nicola called back, but suddenly she was in an excellent mood. She ran up to her bedroom to start packing.

**S NICOLA WAS GOING THROUGH HER DRAWERS** looking for warm clothes to pack, her mom poked her head through the bedroom door. She was still wearing her nightgown, and her hair was sticking out around her head as if she'd just been electrocuted.

"Good morning! Caught any worms?"

"Huh?"

"The early bird catches the worm."

"Oh. Umm, no. Ha ha."

Her mother gave a big yawn and walked partway into the room. Nicola kicked the bag she was packing slightly to one side.

"What does *fortuitous* mean?" asked Nicola.

"It means something happening by accident that turns out to be good luck. For example, let's say one day, on a whim, I decide to take up pottery, and as it happens there is a special promotion where a handsome movie star is giving a kiss to every lady who signs up for pottery. Well, that would be fortuitous. *Extremely* fortuitous."

Her mother looked dreamy for a second, before pulling

herself together and saying, "Your dad and I are going shopping for Grammy's present today. Do you want to come? Or are you too busy? I thought I heard the lovely gentle voices of Tyler and Katie this morning."

"Sorry," said Nicola. "We're busy. We're . . . doing something."

"Oh, okay." Her mother stretched her arms above her head for another gigantic yawn.

Don't ask what we're doing. Don't ask what we're doing.

"So what are you doing?"

Nicola sighed. She was in no way perfect, but she'd never lie to her parents. She knew it would hurt their feelings too much.

"We're taking the spaceship to the planet of Shobble. The commander in chief has asked the Space Brigade to go on a mission for him."

Her mother blinked rapidly. Then she burst out laughing. "You had me for a second there. Oh, you've got a wonderful imagination, Nic! I think you must get it from me. Your father has no imagination whatsoever. Well, have fun." She left the room calling back merrily, "Don't get into trouble on Shobble! Wear plenty of sunscreen!"

Hmm. Nicola was slightly offended. Was it really that unlikely that they'd be going on another mission? Oh, well, it was *fortuitous* that her mom didn't believe her, because now she could leave with a clear conscience.

At ten a.m. on the dot everyone was standing with their bags packed in Nicola and Sean's backyard next to the rusty old swing set.

"Right," said Nicola to Tyler. "Let's set up the spaceship. Do you know what to do?"

"I think so," said Tyler. He squatted down next to the small silver briefcase he'd brought along with him. On the side, it said MINI EASY-RIDE SPACESHIP. Tyler pressed a tiny square button that said ACTIVATE and stood back. "Give it some room," he said tersely, and they all took a few steps back.

The suitcase didn't do anything.

"You've done something wrong," said Greta.

"He has not," said Katie.

"Shall I give it a good thump?" asked Sean.

"Patience," said Nicola grandly, "is a virtue." Everyone stared at her, impressed. Sometimes things like that just came into her head.

The suitcase began to twitch and wobble as though there were a puppy inside trying to escape. It lifted off the ground and spun in circles, slowly at first, and then faster and faster, until it was just a streaky whirl of color.

Everyone stepped back again. There were clunks and clangs and a high *eeeeeee* sound. Sparks flew.

Crash. Thud. Crash.

And there it was—glowing silver and gold in the sunlight—their spaceship.

5

OOK AT ALL THE RAINBOWS!" SHOUTED KATIE.

They had stopped off at Globagaskar to pick up Shimlara just a few minutes earlier and now the spaceship was hovering in starlit darkness over what looked like a tiny, glowing golf ball. Nicola pressed her nose against the window and saw that the glow was caused by hundreds of rainbows shimmering above the planet.

"Aren't they amazing?" asked Shimlara. "I learned about them in intergalactic geography at school. There are a thousand permanent rainbows on this planet."

There was a chorus of *ooh*s and *ahh*s followed by several *wow*s.

"But that's not even the best part," Shimlara continued. "The best part is that ShobbleChoc is made here!"

"ShobbleChoc?" asked Nicola.

Shimlara nodded her head. "It's the most delicious chocolate in the galaxy. They say it's impossible to have a sad thought while eating ShobbleChoc. It's prepared from freshly mined marshmallow and pure chocolate drilled straight from Shobble's chocolate fields. They export it all around the galaxy."

"Not to Earth," said Greta.

Shimlara gave her a pitying smile. "That's because Earthlings get too upset when sales representatives from other planets drop by. They call perfectly ordinary space-ships 'UFOs' and everyone runs around waving their hands above their heads, making it hard to do business. I'm afraid no Earthling has ever eaten *real* chocolate—just that fake, manufactured stuff."

"Prepare for landing," said Tyler into the microphone, interrupting everyone's chocolate reveries. Nicola could see he was rigid with nerves. She reached over and gave him a reassuring pat on the shoulder.

"You're doing great," she said quietly.

"Thanks," said Tyler and his shoulders relaxed slightly. The spaceship began to hurtle toward the planet of Shobble.

As they got closer the colors of the rainbows became as bright as sunshine. Nicola squinted her eyes and saw Tyler take out a pair of sunglasses from his shirt pocket and put them on.

Suddenly the inside of the spaceship was flooded with flickering color: red, orange, yellow, green, blue, indigo, and violet. It was like they'd been plunged into a tropical fish tank.

"It's so beautiful!" Shimlara held out her hands in front of her, as if she could catch the dancing prisms of color.

"Ha! You've got an orange nose!" Sean pointed at Greta.

Tyler cleared his throat. "Welcome to Shobble."

They'd been so distracted by the rainbows they hadn't even noticed they'd landed.

"Great landing, mate." Sean gave Tyler an enthusiastic slap on the back.

Tyler winced slightly and said, "Thanks."

"I think we'll all need sunglasses." Nicola shielded her eyes as Tyler pressed the button to release the hatch and the light from the rainbows became even brighter. There was a blast of icy cold air. "And really warm clothes," she added.

As everyone rifled through their backpacks for sunglasses and their warmest jackets, Nicola went through a last-minute list in her head.

"Wait! One more thing!" she said. She could hear the slight catch in her voice that betrayed the nervous butterflies in her stomach. "Tyler, did you remember to turn on the Time-Squeeze button before we left?" Time Squeeze was an amazing feature that used intergalactic molecular conversion to compress time on the planet you were leaving behind. It meant that the Space Brigade could spend a whole day on the planet of Shobble and only a few minutes of time would pass on Earth and Globagaskar.

"Don't be such a worrywart. Of course I did." Suddenly Tyler was Mr. Confident.

Nicola took a deep breath. This was it. The mission was beginning. One by one they all climbed down the spaceship ladder. Nicola's cheeks stung in the cold. As her feet hit the ground, they disappeared into a soft, fluffy substance that came up to her ankles.

"Snow!" said Shimlara. "I think I remember learning that Shobble has the softest, driest snow in the galaxy."

Nicola reached down and picked up a handful of the white powder. Shimlara was right. It was as soft as feathers and the tiny crystals fell gently through her hand like sand.

As the snow trickled through her fingers she turned her attention upward at the rainbows soaring back and forth across the sky like the arches of a glorious cathedral. If only she'd brought along a camera. She would have to write up a mission checklist for next time.

"Should I pack up the spaceship, Nic?" asked Tyler.

"Oh, yes, good idea."

Tyler pressed a button on the spaceship key. He stepped back and the spaceship began to whirl in slow circles. The circles got faster and faster like a spinning top. Seconds later, the spaceship had disappeared and all that was left was the silver briefcase. Tyler picked it up by the handle.

"Okay, time for some action!" Sean jumped around on

his toes and practiced a few of his karate moves, one of which narrowly missed Greta's head.

"The commander said he'd have somebody at the SpacePort to pick us up," said Nicola. "That's where we are, isn't it? The SpacePort?"

She looked around a bit worriedly. It didn't seem like a normal airport on Earth with the roar of planes taking off and landing, and thousands of travelers hurrying back and forth carrying baggage. Shobble seemed eerily silent.

Shimlara pointed at a sign. It said, WELCOME TO SHOBBLE SPACEPORT—NEVER A MOMENT'S TROUBLE ON OUR PRETTY PLANET OF SHOBBLE.

"Oh good," said Nicola. "Well, I guess we just wait."

Her ears were cold so she opened her bag to pull out a hat.

"What's that?" asked Greta, pointing at a jar in her bag.

"When I was packing I was looking around the kitchen for something useful to pack and I saw this jar of chili on my dad's spice rack," Nicola explained. "I thought it might make a good weapon. I could throw it in someone's eyes." Nicola was rather proud of her resourcefulness.

Greta snorted and looked superior. She reached into Nicola's bag and picked up the jar. "Yes, but you didn't pick up the chili, did you? This is *turmeric*. It wouldn't hurt a fly." Nicola looked down at the jar in her hands and saw to her horror that in her haste she'd actually picked up a jar filled with yellow spice.

"Oh," she said. "Well, anyway, what useful thing did you bring, Greta?"

"Compass," said Greta smugly.

Nicola had to admit that probably was a sensible thing to bring. "What about you, Katie?"

Katie looked slightly embarrassed. "All I could think to bring was my Travel Scrabble set. You know, for if we get bored."

"Well, I brought some *really* useful stuff," said Sean, pulling things out from his bag to show them. "My new Screaming Puppies album in case we need some excellent music, and a bread knife, a loaf of bread, and a jar of peanut butter in case there's a hunger emergency."

"Where's the bread?" asked Nicola.

"I ate it," said Sean happily. "There already was a hunger emergency."

"Great," said Nicola. "What about you, Tyler?"

Tyler winced. "You'll probably laugh at me. I was looking around for a weapon, too, and all I could think to bring was my mom's straightening iron. She's always burning herself on it."

"Well, it's better than a jar of turmeric," said Nicola.

"What about you, Shimlara? Did your mom give you some good weapons?"

Shimlara's mother had given them some great weapons for their last mission.

"Sorry," said Shimlara. "Mom said nothing bad ever happens on Shobble, so there was no point. All she gave me was this instant clothes dryer." She held up a tiny fan. "Mom said that because of the snow, she was more worried about us walking around in damp clothes than anything else."

"Well, I guess that could come in handy," said Nicola, trying not to let her disappointment show.

"I think I can hear bells," said Katie.

There was a musical jingling sound in the distance. Then came a thudding vibration like hooves.

"Oh my goodness, what are those strange *animals*?" asked Greta. "Are they dangerous?"

It looked like a pack of giant chickens was flying across the snow toward them. They were pulling a large silver sleigh behind them. A man wearing a top hat was controlling the reins. Instead of using a whip, he was holding what seemed to be a huge white feather above his head, which he gently brought down every now and then on the backs of the creatures.

"I think they must be ShobGobbles," said Shimlara. "They're native creatures on Shobble and they're very friendly. Gosh, you guys, it's hurting my brain having to remember every single thing I learned in class."

As the sleigh got closer, they got a closer look at the ShobGobbles. Each animal had three intelligent, liquid-brown eyes fringed with long curly eyelashes under one elegantly arched eyebrow. They had tiny kittenlike ears, snub noses, and luxuriously feathered wings that flapped gently by their sides. Their legs were thin and spindly, with large chunky hooves. They were making soft chirping sounds like sparrows.

"Oh, they're beautiful," said Katie, who loved animals.

"Ugly-looking things," shuddered Greta, who didn't. The man in the top hat pulled on the reins. The sleigh came to a stop and he held up a small board with the words SPACE BRIGADE? written in chalk.

"Oh yes," said Nicola after a second. "That's us!"

The man immediately leaped down from the sleigh, lifted his top hat, and bowed. He was mostly bald except for a circle of fuzzy red hair. He was a bit like Santa Claus without the beard: short and plump with round apple-red cheeks, a big smile, and shiny deep-set raisinlike eyes. To her immense surprise he walked straight up to Nicola and gave her a big warm hug.

"Oh!" Nicola awkwardly patted the man on the back. "Hi there."

He then proceeded to silently hug each member of the Space Brigade.

"I just remembered something else we learned," Shimlara whispered quietly to Nicola. "The people on Shobble are the nicest, kindest people in the whole galaxy."

"Can't they talk?" Nicola whispered back.

"Umm, I don't know. I might have stopped listening during that part. It's sort of remarkable that I've remembered this much."

The man was busy writing down something else. It took ages. The Space Brigade all exchanged glances. Finally he held up the board.

HI THERE! MY NAME IS SILENT FRED. I AM YOUR DRIVER. WELCOME! YOU WILL BE WARM AND COMFY UNDER THE RUG IN THE SLEIGH WITH A NICE HOT CHOCOLATE. I WILL TAKE YOU STRAIGHT TO THE COMMANDER IN CHIEF'S COTTAGE. WELCOME! (YOU ARE THE FIRST EARTHLINGS I HAVE EVER MET. YOU LOOK VERY NICE AND NORMAL! DO YOU SPEAK ONGLISH? I SURE HOPE SO!)

"Onglish?" said Nicola to Shimlara.

"It's 99.9 percent the same as English," said Shimlara. "Or 99.6 percent. Anyway, it's almost exactly the same."

"Oh, okay. Yes, we speak Onglish," said Nicola." Thank you very much, ummm, Silent Fred."

Silent Fred gestured at her backpack. Nicola handed it over and he stowed it carefully in a ledge under the sleigh. He did the same for everyone else, and then helped them all climb up into the sleigh.

There were two seats on either side of the sleigh facing each other. Once they were all sitting down, Silent Fred gently spread a big soft white rug over the top of their knees. He produced a red thermos and poured each of them a mug of creamy-looking hot chocolate.

"That smells so *good*!" said Katie.

Silent Fred beamed at Katie and then he took out a plastic container that was full of pale pink, squishy marshmallows. He popped one into each mug.

Finally, he lifted his top hat again, gave another little bow, and walked back around to the front of the sleigh. He waved his big white feather high in the air and brought it down softly on the backs of the ShobGobbles. The sleigh slid gently through the snow with a jingle of bells.

"Oh!" Sean's head fell back against the back of the seat. His eyes were glazed and dreamy.

"What's the matter?" asked Nicola.

Sean said, "I just had some hot chocolate. Taste it. It's . . . it's just . . . *taste it*!"

Nicola took a sip. It was like nothing she'd ever tasted in her life. It was like all the hot chocolates she'd ever tasted before had been pretending to be hot chocolates. This was so much richer, creamier—but it was more than that—it was an entirely different sensation of drinking. Nicola imagined her tastebuds throwing streamers in the air and dancing in the streets.

She looked around and saw similar expressions of dazed bliss on everyone's faces—even Greta's.

"If you think this is good"—Shimlara smacked her lips—"wait till you taste your first bar of ShobbleChoc!"

Soft flakes of snow began to fall. Nicola cradled her mug of hot chocolate in her hands, snug and warm under the white rug. She looked around at a strange world awash with the colors of the rainbows and thought about how her great-grandmother said she had some memories from the year 1930 that were as clear as yesterday. Nicola thought, *I'll remember this when I'm one hundred years old.*

ERE COME SOME PEOPLE!" SAID TYLER.

They'd been traveling in the sleigh for about twenty minutes without seeing a single thing, except for large, flat, snow-covered fields.

Now in the distance they could see a crowd of people walking toward them. As the people saw the sleigh ahead they obligingly stepped off the track and onto the sides to let them through. Nicola could hear their excited shouts as they watched the sleigh approach.

The first thing Nicola noticed about the people of Shobble was that they were extremely dirty.

Some of them were splattered all over with a pink gooey substance that clung to their clothes and faces. They were wearing hard hats and carrying tools. Others were drenched in a shiny dark brown liquid, so all you could see were the whites of their eyes and their teeth.

"It must be the marshmallow miners and chocolate drillers on their way home from work," said Shimlara.

The people looked quite similar to Silent Fred. They all had fuzzy hair and round, chubby faces. Their shoulders seemed slumped with exhaustion, as if they'd been working very hard. However, when they caught sight of the Space Brigade, their faces broke into friendly smiles. They waved enthusiastically and called out greetings like, "Warm Shobble Greetings, strangers!" and "Shobble Joy to you and yours!"

The Space Brigade smiled and waved back. The people of Shobble really did seem especially nice.

They had traveled for another ten minutes when Silent Fred turned around and showed them his board. He'd written: MARSHMALLOW MINE COMING UP ON YOUR RIGHT.

In the distance they could hear the clanking of machinery. A divine smell filled their nostrils. It was like a mixture of strawberries, honey, and rain on a summer's day. Nicola could see the other members of the Space Brigade lifting their noses high and sniffing the air like dogs.

As they got closer to the mine, the smell became even stronger until Nicola's head was swimming. She looked out and saw a hive of purposeful activity. There were hundreds, maybe thousands of miners busy at work. A foreman yelled instructions at a miner driving a forklift. A group of miners appeared from the top of a mine shaft, drenched in marshmallow, and were immediately replaced by another group. "Look," said Sean as one of the forklifts lifted a huge vat of bubbling pink marshmallow and poured it into a waiting container on the back of a truck.

"It's amaz—" began Tyler.

A huge explosion drowned out the rest of his words. The ShobGobbles reared up in terror on their hind legs and the sleigh rocked violently. Nicola clung to the sides, spilling what was left of her hot chocolate on the white rug. She could see a massive ball of red smoke right where the forklift carrying the vat of marshmallow had been. Gradually it cleared and Nicola saw that the vat had been overturned in the explosion. The miners who had been standing nearby and caught in the torrent were covered head to toe in marshmallow. The other miners who had been farther away were removing their helmets and scratching their heads.

Nicola looked back at everyone in the sleigh and saw that they were all covered in tiny pink shreds of marshmallow from the explosion. Sean was busy peeling them off his clothes and eating them.

Silent Fred turned around again with his board. YOU ALL OKAY?

"We're fine," answered Nicola. "What was that?"

Silent Fred wrote, EXPLOSION.

"Well, we know *that*," said Greta. "What *caused* it?"

He shrugged and wrote, DON'T KNOW, but Nicola, who was closest to him, saw a curious look in Silent Fred's pale blue eyes. It seemed to her that he did know, he just didn't want to say.

He turned back around and brought the feather down twice on the backs of the ShobGobbles and the sleigh moved ahead at a quicker pace, leaving the mine behind them.

"I hope nobody was hurt," said Katie.

"Maybe it was some sort of electrical fault," said Tyler.

"They'll have to change their slogan," said Sean. "It could be: 'Just the *occasional* moment's trouble, on our pretty planet of Shobble.'"

"I wonder," said Shimlara thoughtfully, "if that explosion had anything to do with our mission."

Suddenly everybody looked serious. They were all remembering that this trip wasn't just about hot chocolate and rainbows.

Their journey continued on with everybody lost in their own thoughts. After a while they passed another marshmallow mine but this time there were no explosions.

Gradually the countryside became hillier and they began to pass small, humble-looking villages. The homes were small and neat, but most looked in bad repair. It didn't seem like the people of Shobble had much money. If it wasn't for the permanent rainbows splashing everything with color, the villages might have looked quite depressing. The people seemed to be mostly bent old women and tiny children in ragged clothes, who came running when they heard the sleigh bells, their cheeks pink and glowing in the cold.

They passed a giant barnlike building with a sign, DEPARTMENT OF FREE GOODS AND SERVICES. There was a huge CLOSED sticker stamped over the edge of the sign.

"Guess they couldn't afford to keep running that department," joked Sean.

Nicola saw Silent Fred's shoulders move as if he were about to comment, but he didn't turn around.

As they came to the top of a hill, they caught their first glimpse of an ocean stretching out to the horizon.

There was something strange about it.

"Oh!" said Nicola, suddenly realizing what it was. "It's *frozen*."

As the sleigh moved over the side of the hill, they could see huge blue-silver waves snap frozen just before they crashed on the shore. It was extraordinary.

Dotted along the horizon, far out at sea, were large black structures.

"I wonder what they are," said Tyler.

Silent Fred passed back his board. It said, CHOCO-LATE RIGS. THEY'RE DRILLING FOR CHOCOLATE. At that moment they saw what looked like a fountain of chocolate spurt up high in the sky near one of the rigs.

"Looks like we're nearly there." Shimlara pointed at a small sign with an arrow. It said: COMMANDER IN CHIEF'S

COTTAGE. Nicola sat up straighter, wondering if she was going to make the right impression on Enrico.

They could see a big brick wall in the distance. It seemed to stretch on for ages in either direction.

"Looks like the Great Wall of China," commented Greta, sounding so knowledgeable you would think she'd built it herself.

Straight ahead of them was a set of tall iron gates. There was a cluster of people in front of it. Some of them were obviously miners or drillers, while others were dressed in more ordinary patched clothes. They all carried little notebooks and pens. As the sleigh got closer, they jostled about, craning their necks to see who was in the sleigh. Suddenly they began pointing and jumping about excitedly.

"I think they're pointing at Katie," said Shimlara.

Katie finished readjusting her hat and looked up. "Me? Why me?"

Silent Fred turned around to look at them. His eyes widened when he saw Katie.

"What? What is it? Am I turning green?" Katie was panic-stricken. She hated being the center of attention.

"You look perfectly normal to me," Nicola reassured her. Silent Fred pointed a finger at Katie's straight, long brown hair that had fallen out over her shoulders when she took off her hat.

"Her hair?" said Nicola in confusion. "What about it?"

Silent Fred wrote quickly on his board and handed it to Katie.

I'M SORRY. I DID NOT REALIZE YOU WERE A HAIRITY UNTIL YOU TOOK OFF YOUR HAT. IT IS AN HONOR.

"Oh!" Shimlara slapped her hand against her forehead. "I remember now. Most people on Shobble have short fuzzy hair, and it's either blond, red, or black. They call people with long straight brown hair 'hairities' and they treat them like celebrities."

"Well, I don't see what's so special about long straight brown hair," huffed Greta, who had short wavy hair cut in a fashionable bob. She turned to Silent Fred. "It's actually considered quite boring on our planet."

"Maybe I should grow mine," said Sean. "I could be a hairity, too."

Silent Fred held out his board again.

COULD I HAVE YOUR SIGNOGRAPH, PLEASE?

"I think he must mean autograph," said Shimlara.

"Oh, but it's awful! It's so embarrassing!" said Katie. She wrote her name on Silent Fred's board and handed it back to him. Next thing, the people outside the sleigh were all reaching in and thrusting notepads and pieces of paper into her hands, shouting, "Signograph! Signograph!"

Katie signed each one as quickly as she could. Within seconds the whole crowd seemed to know her name.

"We love you, Katie Hobbs!" they called out. "Over here, Katie!" and camera lights flashed.

"This is crazy." Katie's face was bright pink with embarrassment.

"Maybe we should get going," suggested Nicola to Silent Fred, as two young girls tried to climb into the sleigh to have their photo taken with Katie.

Silent Fred, who had been staring dreamily at Katie's signograph, put aside his board and nodded. He stood up in the sleigh and reached for a control box high on the gates. He pressed his fingertip against a panel. After a few seconds a red light changed to green and the gates began to swing open.

"Fingerprint recognition." Sean was impressed.

Silent Fred waved his feather-whip gently at the crowd of people and they obediently stepped away from the sleigh.

As the sleigh moved ahead through the gates, the crowd called out mournful goodbyes to Katie. "Come back soon, Katie!" "We'll never forget you, Katie!"

"Oh, Katie," mimicked Sean as the gates closed behind them. "Can I have your signograph? Can I touch your long brown hair?"

Katie kicked him in the shin, and then said guiltily, "Sorry, did that hurt?"

Sean bent over, pretending to be in agony. Something caught his eye and he sat up straight, forgetting his leg, and looked over Katie's shoulder.

"Wow."

7

THOUGHT THE SIGN SAID THE COMMANDER IN chief's *cottage*," murmured Sean.

Everyone twisted around in their seats to look.

The sleigh was heading up a wide twisting drive toward a grand mansion. It was lit up by thousands of tiny twinkle lights, and Nicola could see flickering fireplaces through large glass windows. After the ramshackle wooden houses in the villages they'd passed, this three-story building looked especially warm and comfortable.

The word *opulent* popped into Nicola's head. It was the perfect plump, sleek sort of a word to describe this place.

"I wonder," said Katie, who had hidden her hair back beneath her hat, "if they purposely describe it as a cottage so the people of Shobble won't feel jealous."

The sleigh came to a stop at an imposing entrance, with wide red-carpeted stairs leading up to huge oak doors. At that moment the doors were flung open and a man appeared, followed by three smiling, fluffy-haired Shobble people.

The man was wearing a long royal-blue velvet jacket with gold buttons. He had a thin, white face and his hair was long, straight, and shining brown, falling to his waist in a thick ponytail. It was like a beautiful horse's tail.

"Another hairity like you." Shimlara nudged Katie.

"The wonderful . . . the extraordinary . . . Space Brigade!" cried the man and Nicola immediately recognized his deep radio-announcer voice. "What a pleasure! What an honor!"

Silent Fred handed over his board to Nicola. It said:

ENRICO ALOISIO, OUR WONDERFUL, EXTRAORDINARY COMMANDER IN CHIEF.

Nicola noticed he'd carefully drawn a little box and smiley faces around Katie's signograph.

As Enrico hurried out to meet them, Silent Fred helped them out of their sleigh. Nicola's feet had pins and needles from the long journey. She tried to get rid of them by discreetly stamping her feet.

Enrico stopped and stamped his own feet in imitation of Nicola. "This is the way you greet people on your planet, is it? How charming!"

"Ummm," began Nicola, but Sean (grinning widely) was already enthusiastically stomping his feet, so all the other members of the Space Brigade had no choice but to do the same.

"For heaven's sakes!" muttered Greta.

As Enrico got closer to them his smile faded slightly.

"My goodness. You're all a lot more—*youthful*—than I expected."

"What we lack in age we more than make up for in experience," said Nicola. This was a line she'd read once in a book, so it rolled smoothly off her tongue. Shimlara giggled and had to pretend to have a coughing fit.

Enrico looked at Shimlara with kind concern. "I hope you haven't caught colds on your journey. Please! Come inside and you can freshen up in your rooms." They all turned to pick up their bags. "Don't concern yourself—my people will take care of your luggage!" Enrico snapped his fingers and two of the Shobble people who had been hovering behind him instantly ran toward the bags.

The Space Brigade followed Enrico inside to a magnificent hallway where they were enveloped in such a delicious warmth they all sighed with relief. There were dozens of glittering chandeliers hanging from the ceiling. Along the walls were lifelike oil paintings in heavy gold frames. Many were portraits of Enrico, wearing various elegant outfits and tossing back his hair, while others showed him with a woman and two children all smiling adoringly at him. There were also some with larger groups of people: dancing at balls, laughing at picnics, ice-skating on the frozen sea. Every single man, woman, and child in the portraits had long brown hair.

At that moment, Katie took off her hat and Enrico caught sight of her hair. He arched his eyebrows. "A fellow hairity, I see," he said, taking her hand and kissing it. "No doubt the fans waiting outside my gates were delighted to catch a glimpse of you. I hope they weren't a bother. All the fuss can be tiresome."

Katie looked uncomfortable. "Why do people think long brown hair is so special?" she asked.

"People think that anything that is rare is precious. Every time I do an interview I try to explain that I'm just a normal guy who likes doing normal things, but what can you do? They never believe it! What can you do?" Enrico shrugged charmingly and sighed.

He gestured to the lady standing respectfully next to him. "This is my butler, Joy. She'll see you to your rooms. I'll look forward to seeing you at dinnertime, when we can discuss the somewhat challenging little task I need you to look after—although I'm sure it won't be a challenge for professionals like yourselves!"

"Thank you, Enrico," said Nicola. She watched him disappear down the hallway, his velvet jacket swirling elegantly.

"Well, if you would just follow me," said Joy. She had fluffy yellow hair like a baby chick and the sweetest smile Nicola had ever seen.

As they followed her up the stairs Joy lowered her voice and said, "I think Silent Fred picked you up from the SpacePort? How did he seem to you? Healthy?"

"He seemed fine," said Nicola. "Is he a friend of yours?"

"He's my husband." Joy's eyes darted about nervously as if she didn't want anyone to hear. "I hope you don't mind me asking, but did you notice if he was coughing? He gets such a bad cough this time of year and he refuses to take his vitamins!"

"He didn't cough once," Nicola assured her.

As they reached the top of the staircase, Shimlara said, "Has Silent Fred always been—umm—silent?"

"Oh!" Joy suddenly looked flustered. "I'm *so* sorry, I shouldn't be wasting your time talking about such trivial matters! Now if you'll just step this way, you'll see there is a room for each of you."

It seemed Silent Fred's silence was going to remain a mystery.

She led them along a corridor with a series of opened doors. Their bags had been carefully placed just inside each door.

"Dinner will be served at six p.m. You'll hear the bells," said Joy. "So that gives you plenty of time to have a warm bubble bath if you choose. Would any of you like me to run you your bath?"

They all stared at her. They were perfectly capable of running their own baths.

"Oh, that's okay," said Nicola uncomfortably. She wondered whether this was the sort of thing servants usually did.

"I should tell you that the commander and his family normally dress for dinner," said Joy.

"Doesn't everybody?" chortled Sean.

Now it was Joy's turn to stare. "Oh, I'm sorry, sir, I mean, they dress *up* for dinner. Quite formal clothes. If you don't have anything appropriate you'll find a well-stocked wardrobe in each of your rooms. The commander said to please help yourself to any or all of the clothes with his compliments. They're all new, of course."

"Goodness," murmured Katie.

"Naturally, there is a bowl of ShobbleChoc in each room, which we will keep filled for you," said Joy. "If there is anything else you need, just dial nine on your phone and a staff member will be there for you in exactly 4.5763 seconds. Please feel free to time us."

"I'm sure that won't be necessary," said Nicola, giving Sean a warning look. It was the sort of thing he'd take pleasure in trying.

"Well, then I'll leave you to relax," said Joy. "I'll meet you at the bottom of the stairs at six p.m. so I can lead you to the dining room. It's an honor to welcome you to Shobble."

She bowed slightly and turned to go. The Space Brigade looked at one another solemnly for a few seconds until Joy was safely down the stairs, then they all said at the same time, *"ShobbleChoc!"* and went running in different directions down the corridor, bumping into one another as they looked for the rooms.

Nicola found her bag in a room right at the end of the corridor. She pushed open the door and walked in.

The room was warm thanks to a crackling fireplace. (Imagine that—her very own fireplace!) Nicola put her old backpack down on the soft white carpet and it looked completely out of place in such plush surroundings. There was a huge four-poster bed with a gold satin bedspread and about twelve fat pillows. She opened a door leading to a marble bathroom with gold taps and a bath that seemed as big as a small swimming pool. She'd never had her own bathroom, either. This was starting to seem more like a luxurious vacation than a scary mission.

As Nicola came out of the bathroom, she saw a crystal bowl on a low coffee table filled with chunky chocolate squares. *ShobbleChoc.* She took a piece and walked over to the window. She wanted to savor her first taste of "real" chocolate rather than just cramming it straight into her mouth, which she was 100 percent sure was exactly what Sean was doing right at this moment.

Even though the room was warm, the window was cold to touch. Outside, it was snowing more heavily than before. It had gotten so dark she couldn't see the permanent rainbows anymore.

Nicola watched the snowflakes drift softly by the window and wondered just how "challenging" Enrico's "little task" was going to be. She put the piece of ShobbleChoc in her mouth and slowly bit down.

The taste of the chocolate exploded throughout her mouth. The marshmallow dissolved on her tongue.

The word *delicious* wasn't good enough.

The word *divine* wasn't good enough.

The word *scrumptious* wasn't good enough.

ShobbleChoc deserved a whole new word made up especially to describe it.

It was simply . . . *divinascrumptiolicious*.

 **MUSICAL SOUND LIKE CHURCH BELLS FILLED** the entire house. Nicola took a last nervous look at herself in the full-length mirror. She had followed Joy's advice and chosen one of the dresses she'd discovered hanging in the wardrobe in her room.

The dress was like something Nicola could imagine seeing in a history book. It was made of heavy red velvet, soft and smooth to touch, with long flowing sleeves and a full-length skirt. Looking at herself, Nicola couldn't decide if she looked extremely beautiful or extremely silly.

Before she'd gotten dressed, she'd taken a long, hot, raspberry-scented bubble bath in a magnificent tub that had a special pillow for resting your head. The only thing about taking a bath was that the steam had made Nicola's hair even wilder and curlier than usual. Oh, well. The bells were getting louder. It was time go.

Nicola stepped out into the corridor and saw the others coming out of their rooms. The boys had changed into high-collared shirts and long jackets. The girls were all wearing long dresses like Nicola and they all spent ages swirling around, paying one another compliments and adjusting sashes and sleeves. Meanwhile, Sean and Tyler fiddled uncomfortably with their collars and sighed impatiently.

"How many bowls of ShobbleChoc did you all have?" asked Sean.

"There was only one bowl there!" said Greta.

"I called on the phone and asked them to bring another one," said Sean. "It was great. Someone was knocking at my door *exactly* 4.5763 seconds after I put down the phone. I wonder how they do that."

"Oh, Sean," said Shimlara.

"What?" Sean shrugged his shoulders. "They're servants. That's their job. So they must *like* serving."

"And how do you know that?"

"Why else would they choose that as a job?"

"Maybe that's the only job they could get!"

"They could get a job in the marshmallow mines. That's what I'd do."

"Come on," interrupted Nicola. "We don't want to be late."

Joy was waiting for them at the bottom of the stairs. "You all look absolutely lovely," she said generously. Then she turned to Katie, with a small worn-looking book. "Please say no if you think I'm rude, but would you mind signing my granddaughter's signograph book? I wouldn't bother you, it's just that she'd be so thrilled and you seem— well, you seem to have a much kinder face than most hairities."

Katie blushed while Sean snickered quietly.

Katie said, "Of course I don't mind." She took Joy's pen and then paused. "What is your granddaughter's name?"

Joy looked confused and a little scared. "It's Polly."

Nicola watched over Katie's shoulder as she wrote:

Dear Polly,

With love from Katie Hobbs xx

P.S. You have a very nice grandmother!

"Oh!" Joy's face was ecstatic. "Oh! She'll think that is just out of this galaxy!"

She stood there for a few seconds looking at Katie's message and shaking her head in wonder.

"Well! If you'd all like to follow me I'll escort you to the dining room."

They followed her as she walked briskly through a maze of endless marble corridors. Shimlara, with her longer legs, kept up easily, but the others had to jog along.

Finally they got to a pair of imposing doors. Joy opened them and then stood to one side to let them pass. "Enjoy your dinner," she said quietly.

They walked into a room with a long dining table set

with flickering candles, silver goblets, and huge gold dinner plates.

"Ah, it is the Space Brigade!" Enrico came forward to greet them, smiling broadly. He had changed into a white ruffled shirt and high-waisted black pants. His long brown hair was brushed out and fell to his waist. A woman and two children followed behind him. The woman seemed to be covered in diamonds. She wore a chunky diamond necklace, diamond bracelets, and diamond clips in her thick brown hair, which was so long it hovered only a few inches above the floor. The children, with exactly the same long brown hair falling sleekly over their shoulders, seemed virtually identical, except that one was a girl in a pink satin dress, while the other was a boy in a tuxedo. "My wife, Carmelita," said Enrico. "And my twin children, Josie and Joseph."

They all smiled identical white-toothed smiles.

"This is the way they greet each other on Earth," said Enrico to his family and he pounded his feet on the floor. His wife and children obediently copied him. *This is getting ridiculous*, thought Nicola as she and the rest of the Space Brigade stamped their own feet, looking embarrassed. (Except for Sean, of course, who stamped his feet so enthusiastically you would have thought he'd been greeting people this way for years.)

"I do hope we've made you comfortable." Carmelita graciously shook each of their hands. She stopped at Katie and held her hand for a few seconds longer. "Ah. Please, do let me know if any of the staff has bothered you for signographs. It is expressly against the rules!"

"The staff have been wonderful," said Katie carefully.

"Please," said Enrico. "Sit! You must be famished!"

They all sat down. Nicola noticed that Josie and Joseph made sure they were sitting on either side of Katie.

Enrico clinked his knife once against his goblet and suddenly the room was filled with scurrying servants all carrying large trays above their heads. Nicola barely had time to say thank you as her glass was filled with something sparkling and her plate was covered with all types of strange, exotic-looking food.

She looked over at Sean, who was looking horrified. He usually refused to eat anything he considered unusual. It was going to be fun watching him try to eat this stuff. Nicola swallowed a giggle and Sean discreetly poked out his tongue at her.

"I asked my chefs to prepare something truly special in your honor for us tonight," said Enrico. "We have piping hot sea-slug soup, the finest oysters á la marmalade, and crunchy strawberry-marinated octopus, with steamed seaweed on the side. Enjoy!"

There were a few seconds of silence as everyone stared at their plates. Nicola noticed that Sean looked extremely pale.

"Yum!" said Shimlara, rather unconvincingly.

As Nicola nervously picked up her knife and fork she saw that Enrico was looking with interest at Shimlara.

"You remind me of someone," he said. "You're not an Earthling, are you? You're much taller than the others."

"I'm from Globagaskar," said Shimlara.

"Ah," said Enrico. "Many years ago, during my army days, I knew a very nice woman from Globagaskar. Her name was Mully."

Shimlara said, "That's my mother. She remembers you, too. She asked me to pass on her regards."

Nicola took a tiny sip of her sea-slug soup. Actually, it wasn't too bad. She took a larger mouthful. It was really quite delicious if you didn't think too much about what you were eating.

Enrico was smiling broadly. His wife Carmelita was smiling, too, although her smile looked more like a snarl.

"Tell me, Shimlara," said Enrico. "I seem to remember learning from your mother that the people of Globagaskar have an interesting skill. They can read minds. Can *you* read minds, Shimlara?"

"No, I can't," said Shimlara.

Nicola knew from personal experience that Shimlara *could* read minds. She wondered why she was lying. It wasn't like her. Normally Shimlara was embarrassingly truthful and said whatever came into her head.

"We don't learn how to read minds until we turn eighteen," explained Shimlara as cool as a cucumber. Nicola would have to ask her afterward what was going on.

"Ah, what a pity." Enrico looked pleased.

The twins, Josie and Joseph, didn't seem especially interested in anything except Katie.

"What are the pupuruzzi like on Earth?" asked Josie, running her fingers through her hair as if she were auditioning for a shampoo ad. "Do they drive you *crazy*?"

"Pupuruzzi?" said Katie blankly.

"You might have a different word for them on Earth," said Joseph. "It's the photographers who follow you around everywhere."

"We call them the paparazzi," said Greta. "But they don't follow *Katie* around. They try to get photos of real celebrities, like actresses and models, and actually you might be interested to know that some of *them* have hair *exactly* like mine."

Josie and Joseph looked at Greta with complete disdain, blinked their big goldfish eyes, and turned straight back to Katie.

Josie said in a low, confidential voice, "I expect she's very jealous of you. That's why she's making that stuff up."

Joseph leaned toward her. "Why do you spend time with these *ordinary* people? Don't you feel more comfortable with other hairities?"

Before Katie had a chance to answer or Greta had a chance to explode, Enrico spoke again. "Well, Space Brigade, perhaps it's time I explained why you're here?"

Nicola swallowed a mouthful of steamed seaweed (quite tasty actually) and said, "That would be great."

Enrico pressed his fingertips together like a church steeple.

"My story begins with a very dangerous young girl," he said.

9

HE GIRL'S NAME," CONTINUED ENRICO, "IS *Topaz*."

His wife and the twins shuddered.

"She's a dreadful, *dreadful* girl," said Carmelita, shaking her head.

"You should see her hair," said Josie to Katie. "It makes me feel sick! It's all wild and curly and all over the place!"

She didn't seem to care that Shimlara had wild curly hair and was sitting right in front of her.

"I love curly hair," said Katie casually. "I always wished I had it."

Josie spluttered loudly on her drink.

"Topaz is the daughter of a marshmallow miner and grew up in a nearby village," said Enrico, ignoring his daughter. "By all accounts, she comes from a perfectly normal family. No one can explain why she has become so . . . disagreeable."

"What has this Topaz girl done?" asked Sean with interest. Nicola could see that his plate was completely clear. How had he managed to eat all that?

"Topaz has nearly brought this planet to a standstill!"

boomed Enrico and slammed his fist on the table so hard they all had to steady their goblets.

"My apologies," said Enrico. His voice became smooth and charming again. "It's just that I'm so proud of Shobble and everything it stands for. Our planet's slogan is, 'Never a moment's trouble on our pretty planet of Shobble.' That has been true for centuries. The planet has thrived and the people have been happy and contented. And yet on the way here, I believe you witnessed a shocking explosion?"

"That's right," said Nicola.

"Well, that was the work of Topaz," said Enrico, looking grim. "She and her nasty little associates spend their days sabotaging the equipment in the mines and the chocolate fields. Days are lost as the equipment is repaired. As a result, there is now a severe shortage of ShobbleChoc. We are losing sales. Our loyal customers throughout the galaxy are turning to inferior products. This can't go on!"

"No," said Nicola. "I see." She was thinking that this Topaz girl sounded even scarier than Princess Petronella. Presumably Enrico was going to ask them to convince her to stop being a troublemaker. It might be difficult.

"But, umm, why?" asked Tyler politely.

"Why what?" asked Enrico.

"Why is this Topaz sabotaging all the equipment? She's not just doing it for fun, is she?"

"Oh." Enrico waved an impatient hand. "She wants the miners and the drillers and the factory workers to be *paid*. Can you think of anything more ridiculous?"

Nicola wondered if she'd missed something. Surely she had misunderstood.

"You don't mean that everyone works for free?" said Nicola, giggling, so that Enrico would think she was joking.

"Well, of course that's what I mean!" said Enrico. "They've never been paid! They've never *expected* to be paid! The citizens of Shobble are lovely, sweet people who have always been proud to work for their planet."

"Oh!" Nicola thought she understood now. "Do you mean you don't charge for ShobbleChoc? You just give it away to all the other planets?"

Enrico looked at her as if he'd never heard of anything more stupid. "Well, of course people have to *pay* for ShobbleChoc. We wouldn't just give it away! People are prepared to pay a premium price for a premium chocolate."

"We charge twenty gold coins plus shipping for one bar of ShobbleChoc," said Joseph proudly.

"Five hundred gold coins for a box," said Josie.

Nicola felt like she was in a math class where nothing the teacher said made any sense whatsoever. If they were making all this money from the chocolate then why weren't the workers paid? She looked at Greta on the other side of the table. Greta was good at math. Maybe she understood.

Unfortunately Greta was scratching the side of her head as if she didn't understand a word, either.

It was Sean who spoke next. "So who gets all the money, then?"

"*We* do, of course." Carmelita turned her head slightly so that her diamonds glinted in the candlelight. "You've no idea what it costs to maintain a house of this size."

"Our family doesn't get all the gold," said Enrico. "Although naturally we get the bulk of it, as I'm in charge of running the planet, which is an exhausting responsibility. Obviously nobody expects *me* to work for free. There are other people who are also rewarded for their very important work."

"Let me guess," said Katie. There was a hint of steel in her voice that Nicola had never heard before. "The only people who get paid on this planet are hairities?"

"Well, as it happens, yes!" said Enrico, with a little toss of his long brown hair, as if this was a matter for celebration.

Nicola thought about all those sweet-faced people they had seen walking back from the mines, their shoulders slumped with exhaustion. She pinched herself hard on the arm to stop the feeling that was rising in her chest.

Normally when she lost her temper she ended up saying something stupid.

She took a deep breath and said carefully, "It just doesn't seem very fair. It looked like the people we saw work very hard. They deserve to be paid!"

Enrico looked baffled for a moment. Then his eyes brightened, he tapped the side of his nose, and pointed a finger at Nicola. "I see what you're doing! You're trying to get into the enemy's head! That's exactly the sort of rubbish Topaz spouts! Well done!"

Shimlara spoke up. Her cheeks were pink. She said, "Actually, I think everyone in the Space Brigade would agree that it's not fair that the workers don't get paid. How do they pay their bills?"

Josie and Joseph made *pffff!* sounds as if they'd never heard anything more stupid. Carmelita yawned slightly while Enrico raised his eyebrows in a superior manner.

"My dear, they don't have any bills! They live on chocolate. They make their own clothes. They are very *simple* folk and they understand that they simply don't have the intelligence to handle the corrupting influence of money. Topaz is simply creating trouble and distress for everyone. And that's why I have called upon the Space Brigade to help out. Now, I assume it's obvious what I need you to do?"

"You want us to try and convince Topaz that the people

of Shobble don't need money?" said Nicola. She was thinking, *We'll just say, "Sorry, we can't help."*

"No, not exactly," said Enrico.

Suddenly his face had lost all its charm and warmth. His eyes looked like hard, shiny, black stones.

He said, "I need you to eliminate Topaz."

Nicola's heart pounded.

"Eliminate?" she croaked.

Enrico smiled the nastiest smile Nicola had ever seen.

"Kill her," he said. "I need you to kill her."

10

NRICO, CARMELITA, JOSIE, AND JOSEPH WERE all smiling the same terrifyingly cruel smiles. They looked like hungry, happy wolves about to swallow their prey. Nicola felt she could actually smell the scent of evil. The other members of the Space Brigade reeled back in their chairs, as if to keep as far away as possible from this strange, awful family.

Suddenly Shimlara's voice was loud and clear inside Nicola's head, although her lips weren't moving. *What are we going to do? These people are HORRIBLE!*

I don't know, Nicola answered, without speaking out loud. *Read Enrico's mind. See what you can find out.*

The other members of the Space Brigade were all looking at Nicola, as if waiting for her to come up with a solution. There was that familiar drilling sensation in the middle of Nicola's forehead she remembered so well from the last mission. Sometimes she thought it might be easier if someone else took a turn as the leader of the Space Brigade.

She sat up straight, took a deep shaky breath, and managed to look at Enrico without flinching.

She said, "We don't kill people. Even if this Topaz really

was a bad person, we wouldn't kill her—and it sounds like she's not bad. She's just trying to fight for what she believes in. We can't help you."

Enrico smiled knowingly. "This is a negotiating tactic, I assume? Rest assured, I'm fully aware of your reputation. The Brigade first came to my attention when I heard that you had survived a trip to planet Arth. I knew then that you must be formidable creatures indeed!"

"But all we did was *freeze* the Arth-Creatures," said Nicola. "We're not killers!"

"Liar!"

This time Enrico punched the table with both fists. Most of the goblets on the table fell over, spilling liquid everywhere.

"Daddy!" said Josie, mopping at her dress.

Enrico ignored her. "I have the *proof* that you are trained killers!" he shouted.

"Proof? What proof?" said Nicola. How could there be proof of such a terrible thing?

He pulled a faded newspaper from his pocket and shook it at them. Nicola caught a glimpse of the headline, NICOLA AND HER FRIENDS SAVE THE WORLD. It was the same clipping that was hanging on the notice board at home. Her heart sank as she remembered what it said. "Oh frizzle," said Sean quietly.

"Let me read this to you," said Enrico. "'Last week,

Nicola Berry blah, blah, blah, and the Space Brigade blah, blah, undertook a daring and dangerous intergalactic mission to *kill* an unspeakably evil alien princess called Princess Petronella blah, blah. *They succeeded admirably.*'"

"But it's not true," said Nicola miserably.

"Not true! It's in the newspaper! Are you suggesting they just make things up?" Josie and Joseph tittered behind their hands.

"I think that sometimes they just bend the truth a little to make a story sound more interesting," said Nicola.

"Princess Petronella is alive and well," pointed out Shimlara. "We never killed her. We just convinced her to change her mind about destroying Earth. Call the palace on Globagaskar if you like. Or call my mom."

Enrico looked thoughtfully at her. He pulled a hunk of his hair over his shoulder and stroked it lovingly like a pet.

"Mmmmm," he said.

Tyler spoke up. "We're just kids, sir. Do we look capable of killing anyone?" He made his eyes look wide and innocent.

"It's true that you do appear very young and weak," said Enrico.

"Hey!" Sean looked highly insulted.

Nicola shot him a "be quiet" look. She decided it was time to press home the advantage with Enrico.

"We're not killers," she explained. "We're more like, umm, *diplomats*." (What a great word to pull out of her head!) "We *diplomatically* solve problems. So maybe we could help you by talking to this girl Topaz and together we could all come up with a solution. A win-win solution. That means a win for you and a win for—"

"*No!*"

Enrico thumped the table again. This time everyone was ready and managed to grab their goblets in time.

"I want Topaz eliminated. That's why I hired you! I don't care if you're not trained killers. You'll just have to learn on the job, won't you? My payment terms are more than generous. You can hardly complain. Look at this!"

Enrico stood up from the table and stormed over to a large tapestry hanging on a wall. He pulled on a cord and the tapestry slid to one side like a curtain to reveal an alcove. Sitting inside the alcove was a treasure chest. Enrico grabbed it and carried it back over to the end of the table.

"This will be your payment," he said.

He lifted the lid. It creaked open slowly. A shaft of gold light beamed straight out from the chest, as if the sun had appeared from behind a cloud.

In spite of herself Nicola leaned forward. She was desperate to see what was inside the treasure chest.

The chest was filled to the brim. Nicola could see

hundreds, maybe thousands of shiny gold coins and the most beautiful pieces of jewelry: bracelets, necklaces, and earrings. There were also dozens of neatly stacked bars of ShobbleChoc, as well as brightly wrapped ShobbleChoc balls, bags of ShobbleChoc marshmallows, tins of ShobbleChoc hot chocolate, and large white boxes done up with ribbon with elegant gold stickers saying: SHOBBLECHOC GIFT BOX. The smell of chocolate combined with the shimmering gold of the coins and the jewelry made Nicola's head swim. There was a feeling rising rapidly in her chest—something powerful.

Suddenly she knew what it was: greed. She wanted that treasure so badly. She could give Grammy one of those gift boxes and a bracelet. It would be the *perfect* present. She could spend those gold coins on anything she wanted—there would probably be enough to put in a swimming pool in their backyard! She could lie by the pool in an expensive new swimming suit wearing those sparkly earrings and eating nothing but ShobbleChoc.

Nicola blinked rapidly and tried to clear her head. For heaven's sakes! It didn't matter how much she wanted that treasure chest. She certainly wasn't going to *kill* somebody for it! Why was she even thinking about it?

Enrico slammed the treasure chest shut and looked at them all triumphantly.

"I expect you've changed your mind now, eh? You're ready to take on the mission?"

Nicola looked around at the other members of the Space Brigade. All their faces were slightly flushed as if they, too, had felt that tremendous sense of greed when they saw the treasure chest, but she didn't need to ask them if they wanted to take on the mission.

"No," she said. "No, thank you. This mission is not for us."

"Oh, what's *wrong* with these people." Josie sighed.

"They're obviously just stupid," said Joseph.

"Shhh." Their mother waggled a finger at them.

Nicola was waiting for Enrico to yell, but he didn't say a word. He pressed his lips together so they made a thin line and walked back over to the wall with the treasure chest and put it away.

He turned back to them. "Well then," he said and clicked his fingers twice.

"Nicola!" whispered Shimlara desperately. *"He's going to—"* At that moment there was a sound of heavy thudding boots and suddenly the room was filled with large, muscular men dressed in metallic black. Their long brown hair was slicked down in oily strands against their potatolike heads. They folded their arms across their barrel chests and stood with their legs apart, looking straight ahead.

"These are my security thugs," said Enrico. "They're the finest thugs in the galaxy."

The thugs nodded and puffed out their massive chests even farther.

"Now, if you won't cooperate," said Enrico to the Space Brigade, "I'm obviously going to need to take one of you as a hostage."

He pointed his finger at the end of the table. "That one will do nicely."

ENRICO WAS POINTING HIS FINGER STRAIGHT AT Katie.

The security thugs went directly to her, lifted her by the elbows, and dragged her to her feet. Katie's face had gone as white as an envelope.

"What are you doing?" asked Nicola, both terrified and furious.

"Get your hands off her!" shouted Sean. He went to stand up from his seat but one of the men put big meaty hands on his shoulders and easily pressed him back down in his seat.

"Hey! This is against the law! I *know* the law!" said Greta, obviously forgetting that they probably had very different laws on Shobble than on Earth.

"Take me," offered Tyler. "Take me instead!"

"It seems I need to give you a little encouragement to complete this mission," said Enrico. "Obviously, your hairity is the most valuable member of your Space Brigade, so she will make the perfect hostage. Once you've completed your mission you can have her back. By the way, we'll also keep your little spaceship somewhere safe for you."

One of the thugs grabbed Tyler's silver briefcase with the words MINI EASY-RIDE SPACESHIP on the side.

"Careful with that!" said Tyler in a panic.

"Take her away," said Enrico to the men.

"No!" cried Nicola. Her mind was working rapidly. The most important thing was that they all stayed together. "We *need* Katie! You're right! She *is* the most valuable member of our Space Brigade. We can't possible complete the mission without her. She is our best, ummm, killer."

This was the biggest lie Nicola had ever told. In fact, Katie tended to zigzag her way down footpaths because she was so nervous about accidentally stepping on ants.

"Yes," said Katie. "I am a highly trained killer." She tried her best to pull a ferocious-looking face, but she looked about as scary as a cranky kitten.

Enrico appeared to be wavering.

"I think it's a trick, Daddy," said Josie. She looked at Nicola with narrow eyes. "Don't fall for it."

Enrico's face turned purple. "I never fall for tricks! Take her away *now*!"

The men lifted Katie by the elbows so that her feet

dangled in the air and carried her from the room.

Shimlara yelled after them, "Don't you dare hurt her!"

They vanished.

Nicola looked over at the empty spot in between Josie and Joseph where Katie had been sitting and made a promise to herself. Once they were all back on Earth, the Space Brigade would retire. This was *not* fun! She wanted to bury her head in her hands and sob with frustration.

Enrico sat back down at the end of the table and sighed, as if he'd just finished something exhausting.

"Well done, darling," said Carmelita, stroking his hand. "This is so stressful for you and you're handling it *beautifully*. Isn't your daddy clever, children?"

"Very clever!" piped up Josie and Joseph.

"Thank you, sweeties," said Enrico, pathetically rubbing his forehead.

"I think I'm going to be sick," murmured Sean.

"Now," said Enrico. "I assume you're ready to listen, Nicola?"

Nicola knew she had no choice but to pretend they were accepting the mission. Then they could work out a way to rescue Katie and somehow get off this planet.

Shimlara's voice spoke up again in Nicola's head. *We're going to have to* pretend *to agree to take on the mission and then we'll work out a way to rescue Katie and somehow . . .*

"Yes, yes, I know," answered Nicola irritably, forgetting that she shouldn't be speaking out loud.

"Good," said Enrico, looking a bit surprised by her tone. "I'm glad you're finally seeing sense! I've prepared dossiers for each of you with all the information you need."

He handed each member of the Space Brigade a thin gray folder stamped with the words TOP SECRET.

Nicola opened hers curiously.

The first thing she saw was a snapshot of a teenage girl labeled TOPAZ. She had the typical Shobble-person round face, creamy white skin, dark freckles like a dusting of chocolate, and very messy, curly red-gold hair. She didn't seem to know she was being photographed and was in the middle of talking angrily to someone, or perhaps she was addressing a crowd. One fist was raised passionately above her head. Her mouth was open as if she were shouting something. Although she was scowling, you could see she had two dimples in her cheeks that would deepen when she smiled.

She seemed beautiful and also very nice.

"She's disgustingly ugly," said Josie, who was leaning over Tyler's shoulder to look in his folder.

Nicola put aside the photo and picked up a typewritten sheet of paper. It said:

THE TARGET:

NAME: TOPAZ SILVERBELL

AGE: 15

KNOWN ASSOCIATES:
    JOSHUA SILVERBELL (YOUNGER BROTHER);
    SERENA GOLDUST (BEST FRIEND)

CRIMES: STIRRING UP TROUBLE BY WRITING
    STRONGLY-WORDED LETTERS TO NEWSPAPERS,
    ENCOURAGING WORKERS TO DEMAND WAGES,
    SABOTAGE OF PERFECTLY GOOD MINING
    EQUIPMENT, ALL OF THE ABOVE = TREASON

YOUR MISSION: ELIMINATE TOPAZ SILVERBELL

NOTE: MAKE IT APPEAR TO BE AN ACCIDENT
    (E.G. PUSH HER OFF A CLIFF—MAKE IT LOOK
    LIKE SHE SLIPPED? A FIRE OF SOME SORT?
    BUT YOU ARE THE EXPERTS.) THERE MUST
    BE NO SUSPICION OF INVOLVEMENT BY THE
    COMMANDER IN CHIEF.

A MAP INDICATING TOPAZ'S BELIEVED CURRENT
    WHEREABOUTS IS ATTACHED.

The map had two small crosses. One said YOU ARE HERE and showed a tiny picture of Enrico's mansion. The other cross said TOPAZ IS HERE. The Topaz cross appeared to be right on top of a mountain called the Cloud-Capped Mountain. It looked like they would have to cross a river, a forest, and an ocean to get there.

Sean looked up from his folder and said, "Can I ask a question?"

"Please do," said Enrico graciously.

"Well, why do you need us to do this? You've got all those tough-looking guys who took away Katie. Why don't you just get them to do it?"

"Well, I would have thought that was obvious," said Enrico. "We are the nicest people in the galaxy. We just don't *do* that sort of thing! Whereas I hear that you Earthlings are *always* doing dreadful things to each other. Of course, I don't approve, but it must be convenient at times, when someone is causing you a problem. I often wish I *wasn't* cursed with such a nice nature."

"But you've taken Katie hostage! That's not exactly 'nice,'" protested Sean.

"You left me no choice," said Enrico. "Desperate times call for desperate measures. People are actually listening to this dreadful Topaz. There could be a revolution. I could be overthrown—can you imagine anything more dreadful or wrong?"

"No, darling, I couldn't." Carmelita pressed a trembling hand to her throat, overcome by the thought.

Enrico continued, "If the people ever suspected that I had anything to do with Topaz's elimination, it could be the end of me. That's why I was so delighted when I read about the services offered by the Space Brigade." He seemed to have forgotten—or was pretending to forget—that he had been wrong about the services they offered.

"Now, I assume you'll want to be off first thing in the morning," said Enrico cheerfully. "The sooner you're done, the sooner I can return your valuable friend. I have arranged for five of our finest, fastest ShobGobbles to be taken from the stables and available for you at the mansion steps at six a.m. tomorrow morning. I have also organized for plenty of provisions for your journey. No, no, don't thank me! I'm only too happy to help."

Nicola, who had certainly not been about to thank him, said nothing.

"Well!" Enrico rubbed his hands together and glanced at his watch. "I think that's everything you need. You must excuse us. My family's favorite television program is about to start."

"It's called *An Inside Look at Shobble's Most Amazing and Beautiful Family*," said Joseph.

"It's a reality TV show about us," preened Josie. "We let the TV cameras into our house for a week to film how we lived. You should have seen how hungry the TV crew looked when they filmed us eating our dinner and they hadn't eaten all day. Oh, how we laughed!"

"Sounds hilarious," said Nicola sourly.

"I prefer to have breakfast in bed, so I won't be able to see you off in the morning." Enrico stood up and smiled his charming smile. "I'll take this opportunity to wish you best of luck. I'll call for Joy to take you back to your rooms. Oh—and please, don't worry about your hairity friend— we'll take *very* good care of her."

His family followed as he flounced toward the door, but then he stopped, his hand on the doorknob. "Unless, of course, you fail your mission. If that's the case, we might become a little forgetful when it comes to delivering her food and water."

He laughed and the rest of his family threw back their heads and laughed loudly with him.

It was the most frightening sound Nicola had ever heard.

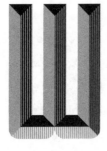

HAT ARE WE GOING TO DO?" SAID TYLER, when Enrico and his family had gone and the Space Brigade was left alone sitting around the long table.

"Okay, I think I've got one idea," said Greta. "What we do—"

"We've got to rescue Katie before anything else," said Sean, who was busy emptying all the food he'd carefully hidden away in his pockets back into the serving bowls. "So first we've got to find out where—"

"And they've got my—I mean our—spaceship!" said Tyler. "Did you see they were carrying it really carelessly? If they scratch it I'll—" He gripped his fists and shook his head.

Shimlara leaned forward urgently. "I've got something important to tell you all," she said. "I was reading Enrico's—"

The door opened and Joy appeared. She put a finger to her lips and pointed at the corner of the room. Then she cupped a hand over her ear.

She mouthed out the words: *They're listening to you.*

Everyone stopped talking. Shimlara clapped a hand over her mouth.

"I hope you enjoyed your dinner," said Joy formally. "Shall I escort you back to your rooms?"

"Yes. Thank you," said Nicola speaking awkwardly as if she were in a play.

They all stood up and silently followed Joy the way they had come, through the corridors of Enrico's mansion.

Nicola was impatient now with the heavy swishing of her red velvet dress around her legs. She wanted to be back in her jeans so she could feel capable and ready for action. They needed to think of the smart way around these people. "Work smarter, not harder," her dad said when he was coming up with a new (and always ridiculous) way to do housework.

Joy led them back to Nicola's room and ushered them in without saying anything.

"Shall I run you a bath, madam?" said Joy.

Nicola was about to say "no, thank you," but then she realized that Joy was nodding her head frantically.

"Oh!" she said. "Thank you. That's just what I need."

Joy walked into Nicola's bathroom, beckoning them all to follow. She turned on both taps at full blast so the noise of running water filled the room.

Then she crouched down on the floor. Intrigued, everyone sat down cross-legged in front of her.

"This is the only way to make sure Enrico's thugs can't

hear us on their listening devices," said Joy. Her voice was low, so everyone had to lean forward to hear her. "Every one of your rooms is bugged. So if you want to talk in private this is the only way to do it."

"They've taken Katie hostage," Nicola told her.

Joy nodded. "I know."

"Can you tell us where she is?" asked Sean. "We'll rescue her." He punched his hand into his fist.

"It's impossible," said Joy. "She's in the hostage room."

"Hostage room?" said Tyler. "This house has its *own hostage room*?"

"Enrico had it specially built. It has twenty security cameras, thirty alarms, and trip wires on every doorway. A team of his security thugs guards it. There's no way anybody could get past them."

"Yeah, this Enrico is such a *nice* person," said Tyler sarcastically.

"Will they treat her badly?" said Nicola. Her heart plummeted at the thought of Katie alone and terrified.

"Not unless you don't achieve your mission," said Joy. "At the moment she's perfectly comfortable. There are books and a television and all her meals will be provided. She's a hairity so she'll get five-star service. But I can assure you, it is *physically impossible* to rescue her."

Nicola sat back on her heels and watched the steam rising from the rapidly filling bath.

"I just don't know what we can do. It seems—hopeless," she said.

Greta lifted her chin. "You shouldn't give up like that, Nicola. It's not very good leadership! Oh, and just a little suggestion—maybe next time you could do a bit more research before you accept another mission from a *psychopath*."

Nicola cheeks burned. It wasn't because the bathroom was heating up. Greta was right. It wasn't good leadership to give up. Maybe she should step down and let Greta take over as leader of the mission.

She opened her mouth but Shimlara interrupted her. Her face was clenched, as if she had a toothache. "I was reading Enrico's mind before. Even if we do achieve the mission, he doesn't intend to let us off Shobble. He knows that more and more people are supporting Topaz and they'll be upset if anything happens to her. So he wants to make examples of us all. He's planning a huge public trial. We'll all be found guilty of murdering Topaz and then he'll put us in something called a 'mobile jail' for the rest of our lives. We'll be taken around from village to village in a glass cage so the people can throw rocks and spit at us. He thinks the meaner he is to us, the more the people of Shobble will love him. He wants to give the people someone to hate—and that will be us."

Nicola, Sean, Tyler, and Greta all stared at Shimlara with open mouths. Even Joy looked shocked. This nightmare was getting worse and worse.

"Oh!" said Shimlara. "One more thing. To ensure we can never tell anyone the truth, he's going to do to us what he did to Silent Fred. He was so pleased with himself for thinking of it. He kept saying to himself, *My extraordinary intelligence never ceases to amaze me.*" She looked questioningly at Joy. "What does that mean? What did he do to Silent Fred?"

Joy's eyes filled with tears. She took a trembling breath and explained, "Once my husband had a beautiful voice. He was the lead singer of the Fleas! That's a famous Shobble rock 'n' roll band. Anyway, one day at a concert he said he was dedicating his next song (which was the Fleas' number one hit, "Rock around the Choc") to Topaz Silverbell in honor of her work on behalf of the miners and drillers. Straight after the concert Enrico's security thugs took Fred away. They gave him something to drink. They told him it was lemonade! It wasn't! It was a sort of chemical concoction that burns your tongue so badly you can never speak again. The last five words Silent Fred ever said were, 'Gee, thanks! I love lemonade!'"

There was silence except for the sound of the running taps as everybody imagined their tongues being burned so badly they could never speak again.

Each time Nicola thought she couldn't be more shocked by Enrico's evil, she learned something new and disturbing about him.

"I guess we could just say 'no, thank you' to lemonade," commented Sean thoughtfully, but everybody ignored him.

"How did such a vile person become the commander in chief of such a lovely planet?" asked Shimlara.

"He wasn't always evil," said Joy. "I've known him since he was a teenager. He was a charming, rather nervous sort of boy, although he did like to get his own way. Anyway, he rose up through the ranks until he became the commander. People adored him! And that's when he slowly began to change. All that power and popularity went to his head. It rotted him from the inside! Yes, rotted! That's the word! He's gone black and evil like rotten fruit!"

The bath was nearly full. Joy wiped a tear from her eye and leaned forward toward them, her sweet face serious.

"You're in a terrible predicament and I believe there is only one person on this planet who can help."

"Who is that?" asked Tyler.

Joy paused, as if she wasn't sure if she should say what

she was about to say. Then she took a deep breath and said, "Topaz Silverbell. The girl you've been hired to kill!"

"Why Topaz? How could she help us?" asked Nicola.

Joy lowered her voice even more. They all bent their heads so close that their foreheads were touching.

"I think the Space Brigade should join forces with Topaz and help her overthrow Enrico!"

13

T WAS ABOUT THREE O'CLOCK IN THE MORNING AND
Nicola lay in her four-poster bed staring into the
darkness.

Stop thinking and go to sleep, she ordered herself.

She needed to be well-rested for tomorrow morning's journey. The Space Brigade had all agreed that they
needed to find Topaz to at least talk to her. Nicola still
didn't know if they should help her overthrow Enrico or
not. It seemed like "stirring up trouble" as her mom would
say. Joy had said that Topaz didn't believe in violence and
was hoping for a "peaceful revolution."

"Oh," Sean had said disappointedly. "Are you sure
about that? Because from what I've heard peaceful revolutions don't really work."

Nicola sat up and punched hard at her pillows to make
them more comfortable. She couldn't stop thinking and
worrying about Katie. What sort of bed was she sleeping in? Was she also lying awake, worrying? *Go to sleep!*
Nicola's mom said, "Worry is the most pointless activity in
the world"—even though she herself spent half of her life
worrying. Nicola closed her eyes tight, but now there was

a strange noise disturbing her. It sounded like the flapping of a bird's wing.

What was that?

Nicola sat up in bed. There it was again—a sort of soft *thwack, thwack* sound. It was coming from her window.

She threw back the covers and hurried over to the window. She pressed her nose against the glass. It had stopped snowing and the moonlight made everything bright and clear against the gleaming freshly fallen snow. There was a man standing knee-deep in snow holding a giant feather and tapping it gently against Nicola's window. Although he was bundled up in warm clothes, Nicola recognized him immediately. It was Silent Fred. When he saw her, he put his finger to his lips.

As quietly as she could, Nicola lifted the window. Silent Fred beamed and held up one finger, as if to say, "Just a minute." Then he took out a piece of paper from his pocket and folded it into a paper plane. He stood back and took aim. His paper plane glided straight through Nicola's window. She picked it up and waved at Silent Fred to show she had it safely. He gave her a cheerful thumbs-up signal and then went trudging off through the snow.

A cold blast of air made her shiver. She pulled down the window and got back into bed. Switching on her bedside lamp, she carefully unfolded the paper plane to reveal a message written in red ink. Nicola knew the handwriting well. It was a letter from Katie.

Dear Nicola,

PLEASE DON'T WORRY ABOUT ME. I AM FINE! I am in a room they call the "hostage room" somewhere right at the bottom of Enrico's house. It's not as bad as it sounds. They have made it very comfortable for me—I guess because I am a HAIRITY. (It's all so silly and I hate that "hairity" word—it makes me think of something my cat would cough up.)

I can imagine that Sean wants to plan a big rescue mission but there is NO POINT. I am being guarded by more security thugs than I can count and they take turns sleeping.

Silent Fred brings me my food so I am hoping he will get this note to you.

I know you and the others will work out some way to convince Enrico to let me out. Don't forget how we convinced Princess Petronella not to destroy Earth!

In the meantime I am trying hard to become friends with the thugs. My Travel Scrabble set has come in handy. The thugs had never heard of the game and tonight I suggested we play it. They loved it! The meanest-looking one with the piggy eyes got a triple-word score and he was so happy! See! I knew it would come in handy!

I know you'll be worried about me but everything will work out fine, you'll see. Say hi to the others.

Lots of love.

Your friend,
Katie

P.S. Try not to let Greta annoy you. Remember, you are the BEST! The Space Brigade would fall apart without you as our leader.
P.P.S. I am cutting all my hair off as soon as we get back to Earth.

Nicola laughed and almost cried. Leave it to Katie to be thinking about other people. If Nicola were in the same situation, she would have sent only one line: *GET ME OUT OF HERE NOW!*

She folded the letter up carefully and put it in her backpack. At least she knew Katie was managing to keep her spirits up.

Nicola lay back down in bed and questions she couldn't answer filled her head.

What would Topaz be like? How much time had already passed on Earth? Was the Time Squeeze working? Should they help Topaz overthrow—

Suddenly, as if she'd just stepped into a deep black hole, Nicola fell instantly asleep.

It seemed like only seconds later that she woke to find the room filled with a kaleidoscope of glimmering color. The sun had risen and Shobble's rainbows were out again.

Nicola sat up, rubbing her eyes. She could hear a strange high sound that was like a cross between a horse's neigh and a turkey's gobble. It had to be the ShobGobbles being saddled up in their stables.

There was no more time to waste. Topaz had to be found at once.

14

TYLER, AN EARLY RISER LIKE NICOLA, WAS ALREADY on the front steps of the mansion when Nicola got there, stamping his feet on the snowy steps to keep warm.

Nicola joined him on the steps, giving him a nudge on the shoulder to say hello. She looked up at the rainbows soaring above them. At this time of the morning the light wasn't as bright and you didn't need sunglasses to appreciate the color-splashed snowy landscape. She took a deep breath. Something about all this beauty made her feel stronger.

"Did you sleep okay?" she asked.

"Not really. I was worrying about Katie and then when I did finally get to sleep I dreamed that Enrico put our spaceship into the washing machine on the power wash cycle." Tyler rubbed his eyes. "I woke up screaming."

The front door of the mansion opened and Shimlara and Greta appeared together, both pulling their backpacks over their shoulders, running fingers through their messy hair, and yawning.

"I had such bad dreams," said Shimlara. "I kept dreaming

that Enrico was offering me tall glasses of lemonade to burn my tongue."

Greta looked around irritably. "I see Sean isn't here yet."

"I hope he's not still asleep," said Nicola, thinking about the times her dad had resorted to spraying Sean with a water pistol to try and wake him up for school.

There was a clip-clopping sound. Silent Fred and Joy came walking down the driveway, leading five ShobGobbles by their reins. Two scowling security thugs stomped behind them.

"I hope the ShobGobbles are easy to ride," said Nicola. She'd only been on a horse once before.

"Good morning, Space Brigade," said Joy. She was speaking much more formally than the night before, obviously conscious of the security thugs listening to her every word. "These are your ShobGobbles. They're fresh out of training school and haven't been given names yet. You're welcome to name them yourselves."

She pointed at the large saddlebags slung on each side of the ShobGobbles' broad backs. "You'll find plenty of provisions for your journey."

"What do they eat?" Shimlara stroked the glossy feathers of the nearest ShobGobble.

Silent Fred held up his board. It said: INDIGO BERRIES.

He'd sketched a little picture that looked like a bunch of misshapen grapes.

"They grow wherever the rainbows shine indigo light," said Joy. Silent Fred handed each of them a large white feather about the size of a baseball bat.

"ShobGobbles are very sensitive," said Joy. "You just brush your feather-whip *very* gently against their sides."

Silent Fred was still holding out one last feather. "Oh," said Joy, looking around. "Where is—"

The mansion doors opened and Sean came skidding down the steps toward them.

"Sorry I'm late," he said. "I had the worst night's sleep. My room was in the middle of Tyler's and Shimlara's. Tyler kept waking me up yelling something weird like, *'At least use the GENTLE cycle!'* and Shimlara kept screaming, *'But I'm NOT thirsty!'*"

"Sorry," said Shimlara and Tyler together. "Bad dreams."

"Now you have your maps?" said Joy. She glanced at the thugs and put on a ferocious voice. "So you can track down that *evil, horrible, nasty* girl, Topaz Silverbell!"

Silent Fred discreetly handed Joy his blackboard. Nicola saw that it said: NO NEED TO OVERDO IT, LOVE. He rubbed it out quickly while Joy looked embarrassed.

"Yes, we've got our maps." Nicola patted her top pocket.

She'd studied the map for ages trying to work out the fastest, easiest way to reach Topaz.

"I've worked out the best way to get there," said Greta. She pulled out her own map and Nicola saw she'd drawn a series of neat little arrows across it. "We head east through the Forest of Thwarted Dreams, cross the Raging River at the Touch and Go Bridge, then go west toward Treachery Bay, and directly north across the Perilous Sea to the foothills of the Cloud-Capped Mountain."

"Uh, okay . . . ," said Nicola, trying to mask her uncertainty. She knew that Greta was much better at geography than anyone else in the group, but some of those places sounded pretty unpleasant.

She took a deep breath. "I was planning for us to head west through the Valley of High Hopes, cross the Raging River at the Safe Hands Bridge, then go east through the Sweet Dream Swamplands, and south across the Honey Sea to the foothills of the Cloud-Capped Mountain."

"That would take *much* longer!" scoffed Greta.

"Yes, but Nicola's way would actually get you there," said Joy. "Nobody ever makes it through the Forest of Thwarted Dreams. They always have to turn around and come back. That's why it's called the Forest of Thwarted Dreams."

"Well, I don't even know what that stupid word *thwarted* means," muttered Greta. "It sounds like *wart*!"

"To thwart someone means to stop him or her from doing something," explained Nicola, trying hard not to sound like she was showing off. (Although on the inside she was giving herself a high five and thinking, *YES! My way is better!*)

"Okay, so we go Nicola's way," said Shimlara impatiently.

Joy was still studying Nicola's map. "Yes, it will probably take you about two days. Tonight you can stay at the Why Not Drop Inn. It's just a few kilometers after the Safe Hands Bridge. You'll be very comfortable there."

She seemed as if she badly wanted to say something else but the security thugs were hovering.

Suddenly there was a commotion from inside the mansion. The doors opened and a flustered Shobble servant appeared, wringing her hands.

"There's a crisis!" she called. "Enrico says his cornflakes aren't crunchy enough! He says they're disgustingly . . . *soggy*!"

The two thugs immediately ran up the steps toward the mansion doors, speaking urgently into their radios. "Code Soggy. Code Soggy. I repeat, we have a Code Soggy. This is not a drill."

As soon as they were gone Joy dropped her formal tone and spoke urgently. "Enrico's spies will be everywhere," she told them. "They'll be sending back information to Enrico. So watch what you say."

Silent Fred grabbed Joy's arm and pointed at something on his forehead.

"Oh yes," said Joy. "One more thing. We don't know how many people support Topaz. Some people think that because Enrico is a hairity he can do no wrong. Others are just so *nice* they think it's bad manners to complain. And of course, everyone is frightened of the thugs. So, if you want to know if someone is a Topaz supporter you can recognize them by this secret mark."

She pushed back her frizzy hair. High on her forehead was a tiny speck like a freckle, but when Nicola looked closer she saw it was actually a tiny letter *t*.

The door to the mansion opened again, and another servant yelled, "All hands on deck! Enrico's toast is . . . *lukewarm!*"

Joy and Silent Fred rolled their eyes at each other.

"You'd better get going," said Joy. Silent Fred helped each of them climb up onto the saddles of their ShobGobbles.

"Good luck," said Joy fervently.

Silent Fred held up his board. It said WE'LL KEEP AN EYE ON KATIE FOR YOU.

Nicola felt like she was very high up from the ground.

She clung on tight to her ShobGobble's back with her knees and grasped her reins tightly.

She noticed that the rest of the Space Brigade were all watching her expectantly.

Whenever you don't feel confident, just pretend you are, her mom had told her once when she was nervous about a speech she had to give.

Nicola held up her chin.

"Follow me," she said, and tapped her feather-whip against her ShobGobble's back.

15

**HOA!"**

The ShobGobble shot off like a fire-cracker exploding. Nicola's head snapped back and her legs gripped the saddle in panic. Cold wind rushed against her face, tearing the breath from her throat and blurring her eyes. She could hear cries and shouts from the other members of the Space Brigade behind her. It seemed they were all having the same trouble. A ShobGobble streaked past hers with someone clinging desperately to its back. She recognized Sean's voice yelling, *"What's your hurry?"*

"Whoa!" shrieked Nicola again, pulling on her reins. "Oh please, please whoa!"

It seemed her ShobGobble was determined to slam them both straight into the wall. She tried to sit up so she could use her feather-whip to guide him toward the gates but it was all she could do to keep her balance. Should she just throw herself off? Which would hurt more? Hitting the ground or hitting the wall?

The wall that surrounded Enrico's property loomed up in front of them. The ShobGobble lifted his head and stretched out his long neck. He was planning to try and *jump* over the wall.

"No!" she cried. There was no way they could make it! Her ShobGobble ignored her. In one powerful movement he leaped into the air. Nicola closed her eyes, leaned forward, and buried her face into the animal's strange-smelling feathery neck.

Suddenly, the roaring sound in her ears vanished. Nicola opened her eyes and laughed with delight.

"You can fly!" she shouted. "I didn't know you could fly!"

Her ShobGobble flapped his huge wings, tilted his head, and gave her a humorous look as if to say, *What's all the fuss about, Earthling? I know what I'm doing.*

She looked around and saw the other ShobGobbles were also flying over the wall. "I just remembered something else about ShobGobbles," Shimlara called out. "They can fly!"

"Yeah, thanks for the warning!" Sean called back.

Nicola's ShobGobble glided to the ground on the other side of the wall. The other ShobGobbles did the same.

"These animals must be untrained!" exclaimed Greta. "Why do they go so fast? I'd rather walk!"

"I think maybe we were too hard with our feathers," said Tyler.

Everyone protested, with comments like, "But I barely touched it!"

"I was last to leave," explained Tyler. "I heard Joy calling out, 'Gentler with your feathers!' Then I heard her say to Silent Fred, 'Oh well, they'll learn soon enough.'"

"We should just fly them all the way to the Cloud-Capped Mountain," said Sean.

"They can only fly for short distances," said Shimlara. "If they fly for too long, they get exhausted and fall asleep midair. A girl in my class did a project on the ShobGobble. I remember imagining how scary that would be if you suddenly heard your ShobGobble start snoring."

"Let's all spend a few minutes practicing our riding," said Nicola.

"But I know I can't do it, Nicola," said Greta. "My Shob-Gobble doesn't like me. I'm not—I'm not very good with animals."

"You'll be fine," said Nicola. "It's like learning anything new. You always think you can't do it in the beginning. Just give it a go."

Greta grimaced and didn't say anything.

Actually, Nicola didn't know if she would be able to work this out herself. She thought about what Katie would do if she were here. Katie loved animals. She was very calm and respectful with them, as if they were people.

Nicola leaned forward and put her mouth close to her ShobGobble's ear.

"Hi there," she whispered. "My name is Nicola."

The ShobGobble was quiet. Nicola saw him looking at her shrewdly with his three beautiful eyes. She lifted her feather-whip. Rather than tapping it, she *stroked* it against his right side as delicately as if she were tickling a baby's cheek.

Nothing happened. Too soft? She was about to try again when her ShobGobble moved, trotting obediently off to the right. *Yes!*

Tyler was right. The trick was to very, *very* gently use the feather.

Nicola decided to risk going faster and tapped her feather a tiny bit harder. After a few seconds, she was able to manage a slightly unsteady up-and-down rhythm. As they thudded through the snow, moving in and out of the colorful beams of light created by the rainbows, Nicola suddenly felt exhilarated. It was like the first time she'd ridden her bike without training wheels.

With a deft twitch of her feather and a pull on the reins, she turned her ShobGobble back around to see how the others were doing. Sean, Tyler, and Shimlara were all getting the hang of it, their foreheads furrowed with concentration.

Greta, however, was sitting astride her ShobGobble and not moving. Nicola rode over to her.

"It's easier than you think," she told Greta. "You just use your feather so lightly it's like you're hardly touching it."

Greta didn't answer. She seemed frozen with fear.

"I'll show you," said Nicola, and before Greta had a chance to protest, Nicola used her own feather-whip to caress Greta's ShobGobble.

"Nico—" began Greta and her ShobGobble trotted off.

"That's it, Greta!" Shimlara called out.

"Try changing direction!" Nicola cried out.

Greta lifted her feather high. It seemed like she'd just keep her arm up forever, but finally, she softly brought it down. Luckily, her ShobGobble obligingly turned the other way.

"I did it!" cried out Greta triumphantly.

"Well done," said Nicola.

"Thanks," said Greta. "And, umm, thanks for helping me."

Nicola was so surprised at this unexpected politeness that she nearly fell off her ShobGobble.

"Watch it!" said Greta sharply. "Your balance isn't that great."

It seemed it was a very *short* moment of politeness.

"Okay, everybody! We'd better get going!" Nicola shouted out to the others. She was about to pull out her map but she noticed a sign. It said 25 VALLEY OF HIGH HOPES.

She pointed to the sign. "That's where we're heading."

"Twenty-five what?" asked Tyler. "Twenty-five miles? Twenty-five kilometers? What measurements do they use on Shobble, Shimlara?"

"You really can't expect me to remember *everything* I learned in class," shrugged Shimlara.

"I'll guess we'll find out," said Nicola. "Let's go." She gave her ShobGobble a gentle stroke with the feather. The others did the same and they all headed off together in the sign's direction.

"You know," said Shimlara as she trotted along beside Nicola, "if it wasn't for the fact that Katie has been taken hostage and we're on a mission for a madman who wants to burn all our tongues, this would be a lot of fun."

OOK! IT'S ALL THOSE CRAZY HAIRITY FANS again," said Sean.

They were heading past the massive iron gates at the entrance to Enrico's mansion.

"They'll wonder where Katie is," said Tyler.

He was right. As soon as the people recognized the Space Brigade, they came running.

"Where is your wonderful and amazing friend?" one called.

"Where is the beautiful and kind Katie Hobbs?" called another.

"They really love her," observed Greta sourly.

"I bet it's because most hairities are really snooty and full of themselves," said Shimlara.

Nicola pulled her ShobGobble to a stop and said to the crowd, "Sorry. Katie isn't with us today."

A rather handsome young boy carrying a single rose fell to his knees, sobbing.

"But where is she?" cried out an older woman plaintively. "I've baked her a cake!"

"I'll have it," offered Sean. "No need to let it go to waste."

Nicola looked down at the pleading faces and thought, *Why should I protect Enrico's good name?*

She spoke up in a crystal clear voice. "Katie Hobbs has been taken hostage by the commander in chief."

There was a gasp of horror from the crowd.

"But Enrico wouldn't do such a terrible thing," said the woman with the cake. "Especially not to a lovely hairity." She looked at the others. "Would he?"

A camera flashed and a microphone was shoved in Nicola's face. An intense-looking woman said, "What's your name?"

"Nicola Berry."

"Nicola, *why* has Katie Hobbs been taken hostage?"

Nicola decided she shouldn't reveal any more. "You'll have to ask Enrico that. I have no further comment."

She tapped her feather-whip as briskly as she dared against her ShobGobble. "We have to go!"

"Wait, wait!" called the reporter, running breathlessly alongside Nicola's ShobGobble. As she ran, the breeze lifted the hair on her forehead and Nicola caught a glimpse of the letter *t*—a Topaz supporter! She managed to push a card into Nicola's hand. "Contact me if you ever want to talk."

Nicola managed to shove the card into her jeans pocket. She twisted her head and saw that her announcement had created something of an uproar. People were gesturing angrily, stamping their feet, and raising their palms high above their heads.

She hoped she hadn't made a terrible mistake and put Katie in more danger.

Her ShobGobble cantered along smoothly ahead of the others, as if he knew where he was going. Nicola squinted her eyes through the rainbows and saw another sign.

▲ 24 VALLEY OF HIGH HOPES.

"That's right! That's where we're going," she said out loud. She realized she hadn't named her ShobGobble yet. She said, "Well done, ummm, *Shobby*!"

Her ShobGobble flattened his ears and made a disapproving snort.

"Oh, you don't like that. Let me think of something better. What about . . . *Gobby Boy*?"

He gave an even louder snort.

"Okay, okay, I guess they're all a little too cutesy. Mmmm, what about *Sky-Glider*?"

The ShobGobble wobbled his head and made a rumbling sort of sound as if to say, "So-so."

"I know! What about . . . *Quicksilver*?"

He gave a long definite chirp of approval.

"Okay, Quicksilver, that's your name. It's very nice to meet you, Quicksilver."

They were now headed diagonally across a vast snowy white plain. Nicola was glad that signs for the Valley of High Hopes kept appearing at regular intervals.

She turned to check on the others. Shimlara had her head close to her ShobGobble's ear as if she were deep in conversation. Sean seemed to be trying to encourage his to rise up on its hind legs, as if he were doing a wheelie on a bike. Tyler already looked like he'd been riding ShobGobbles all his life. At the end of the line was Greta. She was sitting very straight and stiff in her saddle, but at least she was moving in the right direction.

Nicola turned back to the front and Quicksilver tossed his head as if to say, "Look!"

They were passing another Shobble village. A crowd of dirty-faced children came running when they heard the sound of hooves. This time Nicola looked closely at them and saw their clothes were threadbare and their bare feet were turning blue in the snow. Nicola thought of the crackling fires and hot baths at Enrico's mansion. No wonder Topaz thought these children's parents should be paid for their hard work!

She noticed that the ground was beginning to slope downward and snow-laden trees were starting to appear. The next sign they passed said ▶ 5 VALLEY OF HIGH HOPES.

The ground became even steeper and Nicola had to lean farther and farther back in her saddle to avoid falling off. She could hear little shrieks of horror from Greta.

A few minutes later they came to an arched sign that read:

YOU ARE ABOUT TO ENTER THE VALLEY OF HIGH HOPES

"Those numbers on the signs meant the number of minutes it takes to get somewhere," said Tyler, looking with satisfaction at his watch. He scratched his head. "Although how do they know how fast you're traveling?"

"I just thought of something." Sean looked very serious.

"What?" Nicola's heart plummeted at the thought of yet another problem.

"We never had breakfast."

Nicola rolled her eyes. "We'll find a place where the ShobGobbles can have indigo berries and we'll have brunch."

"What's brunch?" asked Shimlara. Sometimes they all forgot she came from another planet.

"It's like a mixture of breakfast and lunch," said Greta in a superior tone. "You have it midmorning."

"Oh! You mean lunfast," said Shimlara. "I always ask the Telepathy Chef for a scrambled-egg sandwich."

"Stop talking about food," groaned Sean.

"Come on," said Nicola. "The sooner we get going, the sooner we eat."

She gave Quicksilver a gentle pat and led the group under the archway.

It was like entering a different world. The light from the rainbows was now filtered through a canopy of trees. Instead of the dramatic shafts of color, Nicola could see quivering patches of red, blue, and green light, as if someone had gone crazy with a paintbrush. It was very quiet and peaceful, except for the occasional soft thud as a pile of snow slipped from a tree branch. The smell of chocolate and marshmallow was replaced by the clean mossy smell of forests and rivers.

As Shimlara had guessed, they were heading down toward the bottom of the valley but there was a wide paved path to follow, so riding was easy.

The weight of worry vanished from Nicola's shoulders. She felt as light and bouncy as a balloon. Anything seemed possible. They *would* find Topaz and work out a way to overthrow Enrico and rescue Katie. Nicola *would* win first prize in the Inter-School Story Competition (even though she'd never actually gotten around to entering), and she *would* be discovered by a talent scout for a starring role in a television series (even though she was a pretty hopeless actress), and she *would* most definitely be picked for the next Olympics (even though she wasn't especially athletic)! Yes! She couldn't wait to see how many medals she would win!

"Guess what, Nic!" Shimlara called out from behind her. "I just realized I'm going to win every single race at the Intergalactic Athletics Competition next week! It's true I haven't been training much but I've got so much natural ability!"

Sean came trotting up on his ShobGobble next to Nicola. "Just thought you should know I'm going to be a black belt by Christmas, so don't mess with me."

Mmmmm, thought Nicola. Sean had only just gotten his blue belt in karate. It seemed like there might be something in the air in the Valley of High Hopes.

Nicola could hear Tyler and Greta talking behind her.

"I'm expecting a letter from NASA waiting for me when I get back to Earth," said Tyler cheerfully. "They'll be offering me a part-time job after school as an astronaut. So I'll be able to give up that boring paper route."

"Well, I was just thinking, when I get back to Earth, I might start a 'Most Popular Student in the School' competition," said Greta. "I'd win it for sure."

Nicola snorted and had to pretend to be having a coughing fit. Maybe this should be called the Valley of *Impossibly* High Hopes.

Although did that mean her own hopes were impossible? No! Her hopes were sensible and realistic!

As they followed the path farther down into the valley,

the vegetation became thicker and the light dimmed. The snow gleamed as if sprinkled with thousands of tiny crystals. Every now and then there was a startling splash of brilliant color from where the rainbow light had crept through. The Space Brigade fell silent. The only sound was the clip-clopping of their ShobGobbles' hooves.

An hour passed.

Another hour passed.

"Chirrrp!" said Quicksilver. Nicola jumped. She felt like she'd been in a trance. She looked around and saw that they'd come to a clearing next to a bubbling creek. A huge pool of indigo light shone on a corner of the clearing and Nicola could see thousands of purple berries—just like the ones Silent Fred had drawn them. Quicksilver smacked his lips.

"Yes," said Nicola. "Indigo berries."

There was also a huge mossy log that looked like it would make a comfortable chair, lying next to the remains of a campfire. It was the perfect spot for brunch—or lunfast.

"Time for a break," Nicola announced and pulled on Quicksilver's reins.

Nicola saw the rest of the Space Brigade stretching and rubbing their eyes as they climbed down from their Shob-Gobbles.

"I feel like I'm in the middle of a beautiful dream," said Shimlara. Nicola knew exactly what she meant.

They led their ShobGobbles over to the creek and the patch of indigo berries. The ShobGobbles took long slurps of water before hungrily attacking the berries.

"I hope we didn't take too long feeding them," said Nicola worriedly. "If Katie was here she would have thought of it sooner."

"I think we've taken too long feeding *ourselves*," said Sean, rapidly pulling out Joy's provisions from the saddlebags. "I can't believe I forgot I was hungry. That never happens to me."

Suddenly Nicola was starving, too. She found a big checkered picnic blanket in her own saddlebag and spread it out next to the log.

"I hope it's not too much weird stuff like last night," said Sean.

"Well, it *looks* sort of normal," said Tyler as he unpeeled the lid of a large silver container. Steam rushed out. He held up something shaped like a miniature rainbow and covered in flaky pastry. "Who wants to try it?"

"I will!" Nicola bit into one. The filling was like nothing she could describe. It was like crunching into a crisp apple at the same time as biting into a piece of chewy caramel. "I don't know exactly what it is, but it tastes great."

"Probably better not to know," said Sean, grabbing one.

Shimlara opened another container to reveal thick jam sandwiches on crunchy white bread—at least they looked familiar. There were also cookies, cheese sticks, gigantic muffins, strange-looking fruit, and bottles labeled INDIGO BERRY JUICE.

"Are you sure that's not for the *animals*?" asked Greta distastefully.

"Who cares?" said Sean. "It's good!"

Of course, best of all, there were also dozens of ShobbleChoc bars and two thermoses filled with the creamy hot chocolate they'd had the day before.

While they were busy laying out the food, Greta efficiently started a quick fire. (It was one of her useful skills they'd discovered on their last mission. She had learned how to do it in Girl Scouts.)

Soon they were all sitting comfortably on the rug, enjoying the warmth of the fire, their mouths so crammed with food they could hardly talk.

A croaky voice that seemed to come from nowhere made them all jump.

"Is that *hot chocolate* I smell?"

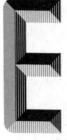

17

VERYONE LOOKED AROUND NERVOUSLY.

"I don't mind you using my kitchen," continued the voice. "But you could at least offer me something warm to drink. I haven't had a hot drink in twenty-three years."

"Is it that *shrub* talking?" whispered Shimlara. She pointed at a short, stout, snow-encrusted shrub in the corner of their clearing.

Nicola gasped as it started walking toward them. *Talking, walking plants!*

"Would you look at all your faces!" the shrub said. "Am I really so old I've started looking like greenery?"

And suddenly it wasn't a shrub at all.

It was a very, very, very old Shobble man.

He seemed to be dressed in a long coat with an ancient black scarf around his neck, but he was covered in such a thick layer of snow you could hardly tell his clothes were clothes. Even his eyelashes were white with snow. He was hunched over, leaning on a stick, and his face was a mass of wrinkles like a withered old apple.

"My name is Horatio Banks," he said. "And it looks to

me like I'm about to meet my first Earthlings! How *interesting*! Just when I thought life might have stopped being interesting, it gets interesting again! You know, I've always been fascinated by your planet, although I've never had the privilege of visiting." His eyes fell on Shimlara. "But if I'm not mistaken, you seem a little tall to be an Earthling. Let me guess! A Globagaskarian, am I right? I once traveled there for business. A very get-up-and-go sort of planet."

"We like to think so," said Shimlara.

"I'm sorry if we've taken your campsite—I mean, kitchen," said Nicola. "Is that where you, umm, live?" She hoped the poor man didn't have to sleep in the snow.

Horatio settled himself comfortably on the mossy log. "This has been my home for the last thirty years," he said. "This log is my armchair during the day and it doubles up nicely as a bed at night. A few newspapers make lovely crispy blankets."

Everyone winced.

"Have a hot drink," said Sean, pouring him a cup.

"And a hot pastry," added Tyler. "Actually have two. Have three!"

Horatio looked amused as the boys fussed about him like grandmas.

"We're the Space Brigade," said Nicola, and introduced each of them.

"It's a pleasure to meet you all," said Horatio. "Mmmm, I'd quite forgotten the glorious sensation of drinking and eating hot food." He took a long sip of his hot chocolate, smacked his lips, and said, "Tell me, what are you all doing in the Valley of High Hopes?"

"We're on our way—" began Nicola. "We're here because—"

She hesitated, thinking about Joy's warning that Enrico's spies would be everywhere. There was too much snow crusted on Horatio's head to see if he had the little *t* mark that meant he was a Topaz supporter. Then again, it seemed like he'd been living in this valley for so long he might not even know that Topaz existed.

"We're on a mission for the commander in chief of Shobble," she said carefully.

"Ah, and who might that be?" asked Horatio. "I'm a few decades behind on my current affairs."

"His name is Enrico," said Greta.

Horatio clapped his hands together and burst out laughing. "Not naughty Enrico!"

"Do you know him?" asked Shimlara.

"I was his teacher. He was a sweet child except for when things didn't go his way. He used to throw the most remarkable tantrums, lying on the floor, kicking and screaming."

"I can imagine him doing that," said Sean.

"And the poor child suffered from terrible phobias," said Horatio. "He had xanthophobia and—"

"What's that?" asked Nicola.

"Fear of the color yellow," explained Horatio. "We had to hide away the yellow paints or he'd end up dribbling in the corner. He also had koumpounophobia. That's fear of *buttons*! He was terrified of them. Let's see, what else? Oh, yes, he had melophobia. That's fear of music. When he threw his tantrums I'd just threaten to sing a song and that would shut him up, quick smart! And there was one more thing—"

Horatio frowned at the sandwich Shimlara had just given him and then he snapped his fingers. "He had arachibutyrophobia. That's fear of peanut butter sticking to the roof of his mouth. Tell me, does he still suffer from all those phobias?"

"I don't know," said Nicola. "He is quite . . . strange."

"I always told him that he needed to stop letting his phobias rule his life but he wouldn't listen. And now the little scamp is in charge of Shobble, eh? Does he do a good job?" Horatio took a massive bite of the sandwich.

"Well," said Nicola. "We're from another planet so we don't really know, but the thing is, the marshmallow miners and chocolate drillers don't get paid for their work."

"They don't need any money," said Horatio cheerfully.

"They just go along to the Department of Free Goods and Services for anything they need—clothing, building materials, medicine, food other than chocolate. It's an enormous building. You just wheel your trolley about and help yourself! Wonderful place."

Nicola thought back to the building they'd gone past when they first arrived in Shobble.

"I think Enrico closed it," said Nicola.

"Oh." Horatio's bushy eyebrows drew together to form a v shape. "But then what does he do with all the money from the sales of ShobbleChoc?"

"He spends it on himself and his family and other hairities," said Greta.

"What's a hairity?" asked Horatio.

"It's someone with long straight brown hair," explained Nicola. "They're like celebrities on this planet. People take photos of them."

Horatio clapped his hands together. "What a turnaround for the books! Once upon a time children would make fun of people with long brown hair just because they were unusual. Enrico, for example, was teased terribly at school about his hair. He used to get very upset." Horatio paused. He seemed to be thinking. "Perhaps that's what this is all about. Naughty Enrico is taking revenge on all those people who teased him at school."

"I thought Shobble people were the nicest people in the galaxy," said Shimlara. "Why did the other children tease him?"

"Well, I must admit that's something of a myth we do like to encourage. While we are extremely nice, easygoing people, there are exceptions to every rule," said Horatio. "But tell me—why are the people of Shobble putting up with this shabby treatment by naughty Enrico?"

"It's not that easy to get rid of a commander in chief," said Nicola, thinking of Enrico's huge security thugs.

"Oh, I shouldn't think it would be that much trouble," said Horatio airily.

The members of the Space Brigade exchanged looks that meant, *Huh, what does he know?!*

"I know what you're thinking," said Horatio. "You're thinking he's just an old man, what would he know?"

"Oh, no, not all!" they all protested.

"Well, I actually know quite a lot," said Horatio. "My great-grandmother was one of the people who helped draft Shobble's constitution. I know every word of the constitution by heart. You might be interested in clause number 367-AAB-38479579034554. Shall I recite it to you?"

"All right," said Nicola, hoping it wouldn't take too long. They really needed to get going soon.

"If enough Shobble people sign a petition on a length of

rose-colored parchment, calling politely and respectfully for the removal of a commander in chief, and that parchment is long enough to stretch the length of a Shobble rainbow, then the commander must resign gracefully and immediately, whereupon an election must be held for a new commander. An attractive thank-you card should be sent to the resigning commander within fourteen days."

The Space Brigade all stared at Horatio. Surely it couldn't be that easy.

"My great-grandmother was a stickler for good manners," said Horatio. "That's why there is all that stuff about 'politely' and 'respectfully.'"

"But Enrico would just ignore the constitution," said Sean. "Or maybe he's even changed that rule already."

"Nobody can change the constitution," said Horatio. "That's clause number 1739-ZZZZ-1749237937432798489, which says 'The constitution is perfect, thanks very much, and cannot and shall not ever be changed.' And the constitution certainly cannot be ignored, even by naughty Enrico. The little rogue!"

"Well," said Nicola doubtfully. She could so easily imagine Enrico curling his lip and saying he was far too important for the constitution to apply to him. "But why hasn't anyone thought of this before?"

"I expect because the constitution takes up over two

thousand volumes and nobody can be bothered to read it all," said Horatio.

Suddenly Nicola was filled with hope. *This will solve everything. This mission will be as easy as pie! We'll just arrange for a petition as long as a rainbow calling for Enrico's resignation!*

She shook herself.

"Why does this valley make you feel so hopeful?" she asked Horatio.

"They say that it's this particular species of tree." Horatio pointed out a gnarled old tree with fat purple leaves. "It's called the Hope Tree. Apparently it creates a chemical that triggers a feeling of hopefulness."

"So it's not real," said Greta, looking disappointed.

"Oh, hopes are always real," said Horatio. "It's just that most of the time we try to squish them down. In the valley, our hopes are allowed to grow and flourish—like they should!"

As they were packing up their picnic, Shimlara said to Horatio, "May I ask you a question, Horatio?"

"Certainly."

"Why do you live here in the valley all alone? Don't you have a family?"

"I had a falling out with my family many years ago," said Horatio. "There was a terrible argument over the merits of milk chocolate versus dark chocolate. Unforgivable things were said—mostly by me. I stormed off in a huff one stormy night and ended up here."

Horatio's face was filled with despair as he remembered that night. Then suddenly it cleared as though the sun had come out. "But I know that one day my family will forgive me. Just when I least expect it, they'll turn up and tell me it's time to come home."

"But Horatio, wouldn't it be better if you went and apologized to your family?" said Nicola. "They might not even know where you are!"

"Nonsense." Horatio settled himself back down on his log. "I'm sure they'll be along any minute! Don't worry about me!"

Nicola realized there was nothing she could say. She looked around at the others, who were climbing up onto their well-rested ShobGobbles. Everyone shrugged slightly.

Quicksilver pawed at the ground. It was time for their journey to continue.

18

OBODY IN THE SPACE BRIGADE SAID ANYTHING as they once again followed the paved path through the Valley of High Hopes.

Ridiculously hopeful thoughts continued to creep into Nicola's head.

I expect I'll win a trip to Disneyland soon. Maybe in a raffle. Or I might find the winning ticket in a cereal box.

I bet they'll stop teaching math in school soon. It's not like anybody likes it—except for the people who are good at it—and they don't need to learn it, anyway!

"I think we must have reached the bottom of the valley," Tyler called out. "We seem to be heading up again."

He was right. Nicola could feel it was more of an effort for Quicksilver as the path ahead became steeper. She stroked the creature's feathery mane to show her appreciation.

An hour passed and the light was becoming brighter.

"I can smell chocolate again," said Sean, sniffing deeply.

Nicola saw an archway ahead with a sign. As they got closer, she read:

THANK YOU FOR VISITING THE VALLEY OF HIGH HOPES.
MAY YOUR HOPES CONTINUE TO FLY HIGH . . .
COME AGAIN!

The ShobGobbles trotted under the archway and suddenly the members of the Space Brigade were all squinting, blinking, and reaching for their sunglasses as they came out into the sunlight and the blinding colors of the rainbows.

Nicola's sunglasses were looking a bit out-of-date compared to Greta's oversized movie-star pair. *I'll have to get some new ones before I compete in the Olympic Games,* she thought. *After all, I'll have all those television cameras— wait a second!* Suddenly she realized there was no way in the world she was going to be an Olympic athlete. That was just a crazy fantasy created by the Hope Tree and its powerful chemicals. She let out a little sigh as she let all those crazy hopes drift away.

"Let me check the map," she called out to the others.

Everyone pulled up their ShobGobbles while Nicola took out the map.

"Next we cross the Raging River at the Safe Hands Bridge," she said.

"I can't see any sign for the Raging River," said Shimlara.

"Neither can I," said Nicola. "I guess we'll just have to

head west. So that would be, ummm—" She looked up help-lessly at the rainbows arching over them. Which way was west? She had absolutely no idea.

"We need a compass," said Tyler.

"Ahem," said Greta. They all turned to look at her. She was holding her compass up high. "Luckily some of us packed something *useful*."

"Oh, well done," said Nicola, wishing she'd been the one to bring a compass.

"Don't worry, Nic," said Sean. "I'm sure your jar of tur-meric will come in useful soon."

Nicola made a face at him.

Greta studied the compass with a deadly serious ex-pression on her face for ages, until Sean said, "Are you sure you know what you're doing?"

"Of course I do," snapped Greta. "Unlike Nicola, I have brilliant navigational skills." She looked up from the compass and pointed in a diagonal direction to her left. "That way."

"Good," said Nicola. She looked at her watch. "We should try and go a bit faster. We don't want to be crossing the river in the dark."

Nicola saw Sean give her a grin of understanding.

"Will you be all right going a bit faster, Greta?" Nicola asked innocently.

"I'll be fine," said Greta grimly.

Nicola tapped her feather as hard as she dared and Quicksilver responded by breaking into such a fast gallop Nicola was sure she would fall. *That would make Greta completely unbearable.*

After a few seconds she managed to get her rhythm back and start to enjoy the sensation of pelting across a snowy field, the air rushing against her face. They passed another marshmallow mine, a village, and a ramshackle old school.

A few minutes later, she saw a sign saying RAGING RIVER with an arrow pointing straight ahead. They pounded along, going up a small hill where Nicola caught a glimpse of a frozen sea in the distance before plunging down again, following a winding track in and out of huge gray tree trunks that soared as high as the arches of the rainbows.

There was a sound of rushing water.

"Whoa!" She pulled on Quicksilver's reins. "I think we're here."

Nicola looked with fascination at the river in front of her. She'd never seen such angry, powerful-looking water. It frothed and boiled and bubbled. It was like water bursting from a fireman's hose. There was no way you could swim in it; it would toss you about and tear you to pieces.

The river was so wide Nicola couldn't see the other shore. She looked around for the Safe Hands Bridge. There it was—a thin, rickety-looking bridge that seemed to be held up by string.

"It doesn't look like you'd be in especially safe hands crossing that," commented Shimlara as she and Sean pulled up on either side of Nicola.

"Let's just fly the ShobGobbles across," said Sean.

Nicola noticed Quicksilver tense up and flatten his ears.

"I think it's too far for them," she said and Quicksilver relaxed.

Tyler arrived next. "You wouldn't want to fall in there," he said, looking at the river nervously. He wasn't a confident swimmer and always stayed at the shallow end of the pool.

They all turned around to look for Greta. She pulled up beside them a minute later, her face bright red. "I'm sure we didn't *really* need to go that fast," she said.

As they headed toward the bridge they came across a bearded, toothless man sitting in a picnic chair with his feet up on a long table in front of him.

"Shock-Sticks! Shock-Sticks! We've got the best quality Shock-Sticks on Shobble!" chanted the man when he saw them.

"What are Shock-Sticks?" Sean asked the man.

"Well, they're to protect yourselves from the Biters, of course, young fella," said the man. "The river is chock-full of them."

"What's a Biter?" asked Nicola.

The man chuckled. "Oh, come on now, don't you be pretending a smart-looking girl like you has never heard of a Biter. I won't be falling for that."

"We really don't know," said Nicola. "We come from another planet."

"Well, if you really want to know, go and read that sign over there." The man gestured at a small wooden sign near the bridge. He peered up at her. "Hey, do I know you from somewhere?"

"I don't think so," said Nicola.

"Biters," said Sean as they rode their ShobGobbles over toward the sign. "I wonder if they're like mosquitoes."

When they got to the sign, they all read it silently together.

WARNING!

THIS RIVER IS HOME TO THE NATIVE BITER. BITERS ARE RIVER-
DWELLING CREATURES ABLE TO GROW TO TWENTY FEET IN LENGTH.
AN ADULT BITER HAS OVER TWO THOUSAND RAZOR-SHARP
TEETH AND IS ABLE TO LEAP OVER A HUNDRED FEET IN THE AIR.
ALTHOUGH THEY ARE HERBIVORES, BITERS ENJOY ATTACKING

HUMANS OF ALL SHAPES AND SIZES. THEY TAKE LARGE BITES AND THEN IMMEDIATELY SPIT OUT THE BLOODY FLESH (ALMOST WITH DISGUST). AS THE NORMAL HABITAT OF THE BITER IS DARK, MURKY, AND UNDERWATER, THEY ARE EXTREMELY SURPRISED WHEN A WHITE LIGHT IS SHONE IN THEIR EYES. THIS HAS LED TO THE DEVELOPMENT OF THE SHOCK-STICK—AN EFFECTIVE FORM OF PROTECTION AGAINST THE BITER. TO AVOID UPSETTING FATALITIES, ANYONE CROSSING THE SAFE HANDS BRIDGE SHOULD CARRY A SHOCK-STICK AT ALL TIMES.

"They don't sound much like mosquitoes," said Sean.

**E DON'T HAVE ANY MONEY TO BUY SHOCK-**
Sticks," said Nicola.

"But the Shobble people don't get paid for anything," Shimlara reminded her.

They had left their ShobGobbles snacking on more indigo berries and were heading back to the bearded, toothless man who now had his head buried in a newspaper. "Excuse me," said Nicola.

The man looked up and his eyes flew from Nicola to the newspaper and back again.

"I knew I recognized you!" he said triumphantly. He turned the newspaper around. On the front page of the newspaper was a large photo of Nicola sitting astride Quicksilver. The headline read:

EARTHLING SAYS, "ENRICO TOOK KATIE HOBBS HOSTAGE."

Comment from the Commander's Press Office: ABSOLUTE GARBAGE.

STORY BY JENNY JENKINS

Nicola read the first paragraph of the article.

A spokesperson for Enrico strenuously denied the Earthling's allegation that the visiting hairity, Katie Hobbs, had been taken hostage. "Why would we take Katie hostage?" he said. "She is Enrico's special guest. The Earthling must have rocks in her head." This reporter is interested to note, however, that Katie herself was not available for comment. Could our much-loved commander be bending the truth?

Oh dear, thought Nicola. Enrico wasn't going to be happy about this bad publicity. What had she been thinking? She should have kept her mouth shut.

"You really should have kept your mouth shut, Nicola," said Greta, leaning over Nicola's shoulder to read the story.

"So is it true?" asked the man. As he leaned forward to hear Nicola's answer, he tipped back his straw hat, revealing his forehead and a tiny tattoo of the letter *t*. Nicola relaxed—he was a Topaz supporter.

"Yes," answered Nicola.

"But why would the commander do that?"

"He's trying to force us to kill Topaz Silverbell," said Nicola. "But don't worry, we would never hurt Topaz!"

"Well, that's a relief!" said the man. He put the newspaper to one side. "I'm assuming you'd all like to arm yourselves with Shock-Sticks before you cross the river?"

"Yes," said Nicola. "But we're not sure how we pay you."

"No need for money!" said the man cheerily. "Haven't you heard? The Shobble people are the nicest people in the galaxy."

He handed each of them a long thin stick made out of a hard gold material. It was about the length of a baseball bat. There were two buttons at one end of the stick labeled SHOCK and RETREAT.

"Let me show you how it works," said the man.

He held out the Shock-Stick in front of him like a sword and pressed the button marked SHOCK. The stick sprang out so it was at least triple its length. There was a bright white light at the end.

"I recommend yelling 'Gotcha!' at the same time," said the man. "Just my little tip. I think it adds to the shock value. Make sure the light shines directly into the Biter's eyes. Then just press the RETREAT button." The stick sprang back to its previous size. "Easy, eh?"

"What if a biter comes at you from behind?" asked Shimlara.

"It's advisable to watch each other's backs when you're crossing the bridge."

"What if you're the last one in the line?"

"Try not to be!" chortled the man. "Or put your least favorite person last!" He handed each of them a Shock-Stick. "Good luck! I'm sure you'll all make it across the bridge. Or most of you, anyway. Ha ha!"

The Space Brigade gave him sickly smiles.

They headed back to the ShobGobbles, holding on tightly to their Shock-Sticks.

"I'll go last," said Nicola bravely.

"I should go last because I'm the tallest," said Shimlara.

"That's exactly why you shouldn't go last!" said Nicola. "You'll be a target for the Biters."

"I should go last because I'm the oldest," said Sean.

"Well, I should go last, because, um, I wear glasses," said Tyler.

"What's that got to do with anything?" said Greta. "I should go last because I'm the least favorite person."

There was a stunned silence. Everybody turned to look at Greta in shock and embarrassment. It was actually true—but it wasn't the sort of thing you were meant to say out loud. Nicola felt terrible. Imagine being in a group where you knew you were the least popular person.

Greta shrugged. "It's fine. I'm really popular in other groups, like my math club. It's just that you people don't really *get* me."

Nicola said sternly, "You are *not* the least favorite

person. I'm going last because I'm the leader and that's all there is to it. Shimlara, you can be first."

Silently, they all climbed back onto their ShobGobbles, their feather-whips and Shock-Sticks held nervously aloft. With Shimlara leading the way, they clip-clopped toward the Safe Hands Bridge.

"Just remember, we're doing this for Katie!" Nicola called out as their ShobGobbles began to cross the bridge in single file.

She tried not to look at the water below. The bridge swayed back and forth as if they were on a ship.

Shimlara screamed.

The first Biter had shot straight up into the air from the river below and was heading for her neck. Nicola caught a glimpse of a sleek wet body, an unspeakably evil mouth, and tiny cruel eyes.

"Gotcha!" cried Shimlara and pressed the button on her Shock-Stick. At the sight of the bright white light, the Biter recoiled and dropped straight back into the river like a falling stone.

"Easy-peasy!" cried Shimlara, although her voice sounded a bit strained.

They continued on for several minutes without anything happening. Nicola felt her shoulders relax. Shimlara must have frightened off the Biters. They were now about halfway across. Sean turned around in his saddle to grin back at Nicola.

He said, "Looks like Shimlara will be the only one who gets to use her Shock-Stick."

"No need to be disappointed," said Nicola.

"I'm not," said Sean unconvincingly. "I'm just saying—" His eyes widened and suddenly he released his Shock-Stick at a point just above Nicola's head and yelled, *"Gotcha!"*

"No need to thank—" began Sean.

"Gotcha!" screamed Nicola. She pressed the SHOCK button on her Shock-Stick just in time to stun the Biter that had been about to sink its teeth into Sean's leg.

Suddenly the air around them was filled with dark flying shapes. Nicola didn't even have time to feel frightened. She was ducking, weaving, twisting to the left, then the right, as she thrust her Shock-Stick this way and that like a sword fighter. As fast as one Biter fell back into the river, another one leaped into the air to take its place. Some of them got so close Nicola felt their clammy, fishy flesh brush against hers. She didn't need to look at her Shock-Stick to find the buttons. Her thumb automatically zipped back and forth between the two buttons. *Shock. Retreat. Shock. Retreat.*

"Yes!"

It was a triumphant shout from Shimlara. Nicola looked

up and saw that she'd safely reached the other shore. Next was Greta, followed by Tyler and Sean.

Quicksilver surged forward impatiently. *"Nicola!"*

Nicola had lost concentration. She swung her head and glimpsed the deadly shape of a determined Biter. It was too late for her Shock-Stick. Cruel teeth sank into the flesh of her arm. Nicola yelled out in pain and fear and tried to jerk her arm away, losing her balance.

She gripped her knees desperately, trying to right herself, but it was too late. At that moment, the bridge swerved violently and she was flung straight off Quicksilver's back.

Arms and legs flailing, she fell straight into the icy waters below.

20

THE RIVER WAS SO COLD IT WAS LIKE BEING punched in the stomach. Nicola gasped for air and swallowed water instead.

Choking and sputtering, she tried to swim, but the pull of the water was too powerful. She was being carried away like a helpless twig. She looked up and saw the shore in front of her rapidly disappearing.

Suddenly there was a frantic chirping sound.

Quicksilver!

He was flying down as low as he could alongside her, his wings splashing the water, his three eyes bright with concern. Nicola grabbed on hard to his feathery side.

With a grunt of pain, she somehow managed to haul herself out of the water and back into the saddle. She fell forward against his neck, exhausted by the effort, her arm aching, as Quicksilver flew back into the air.

There were shouts of encouragement from the Space Brigade standing on the shore near the bridge. Nicola lifted her chin wearily and saw that Quicksilver had rescued her from the very middle of the river.

"Can you fly this far?" she wondered out loud.

She saw that Quicksilver's wings were already flapping slowly.

"No, no, don't fall asleep!" she said.

Quicksilver's eyelids drooped. His head tipped forward and he pulled it back a few times as if he were trying not to slide into a beautiful, restful sleep.

Nicola saw they were losing height. What could she do? She did *not* want to end up in that river again.

She put her mouth close to Quicksilver's ear and made a sound like an alarm clock. *"Brrrrrrrrrrrrr!"*

Quicksilver's head jerked and they rose back up into the air.

Desperate to keep him awake, Nicola began to sing the words to an annoying cat-food commercial. (She was not a great singer.) Quicksilver's ears twitched irritably. He gave her a rather reproachful look, took a deep breath, and flew straight to the shore, landing clumsily in a flurry of snow. His legs folded beneath him, his head fell to one side, and seconds later he was snoring: a loud, rumbling, very human sort of snore. Weak with relief, Nicola slid off Quicksilver's saddle onto the snow and leaned back against his warm, feathery flank. She looked down at her arm and saw blood seeping through a tear in her jacket and sweater.

Sean got to Nicola first and knelt down beside her. He lifted her arm.

"That's a massive bite," he said admiringly.

"Press this against it." Greta pulled a crisp white hanky from her pocket. "Just make sure you wash it before I get it back. Actually, you might have to buy me a new one."

"Is that an ambulance I hear?" asked Shimlara.

"It's not an ambulance," said Tyler. "It's a person!" He pointed toward a figure jogging purposefully out of the woods. She was wearing a pair of blue overalls with the words BITER WOUND UNIT embroidered on the front and a big satchel hung over her side. A flashing revolving blue light was attached to her forehead by a headband. As she got closer, everyone clapped their hands over their ears. The woman switched the siren off.

"Hello there. Sorry about the noise. I'm so used to it I forget it's rather loud. I'm Barb. What have we got here?"

Barb knelt down beside Nicola and lifted her arm. "You poor thing."

Nicola stared up at her. There was something about Barb. It had to do with the little *v* shape in between her eyes when she frowned.

Something important.

"Horseradish," said Nicola.

No, that wasn't the word she'd meant to say.

"I beg your pardon?" said Barb.

Nicola felt as though someone was rolling her up in a big blanket of nothingness.

Everything went black.

21

**ICOLA'S EYES FLUTTERED OPEN AND THE FIRST** thing she saw was an open window revealing a bright splash of overlapping rainbows. She was still on Shobble, lying in bed in a small room with wooden floors. The walls were blank except for one picture of an imposing-looking mountain with a caption that read: *Summer's morning, The Cloud-Capped Mountain, The Planet of Shobble.*

That's where Topaz was. Would they ever reach her? It already felt like weeks since they'd left Enrico's mansion, when in fact it was only . . . ? Nicola was confused. Yesterday?

The door to her room burst open and in came Shimlara precariously carrying a tray filled with food.

As Nicola pushed herself up to a sitting position Shimlara placed the tray in front of her. "How are you feeling?"

Nicola pushed back her pajama sleeve and saw that there was a white gauze bandage wrapped neatly around her upper arm. Besides a dull ache, it didn't hurt at all.

"Barb had to give you ten stitches," said Shimlara. "Luckily you were already unconscious."

"Where are we?" Nicola picked up the spoon and began to eat something that looked like porridge and tasted of cinnamon and apple.

"We're at the Why Not Drop Inn," said Shimlara.

"And we got here last night?" asked Nicola. She felt like she had fallen asleep halfway through a movie, only the movie was her life.

There was a knock on the door.

"Come in," said Nicola.

It was Barb, in a freshly ironed pair of blue overalls with her siren strapped around her head. "I thought I'd check in on my patient," she said.

"I'm feeling good," said Nicola. "Thank you very much for everything that you did."

"Let's take a quick look at that bite," Barb said as she sat down on the bed. As she unwound the bandage from Nicola's arm, she frowned.

"Horatio!" cried Nicola excitedly. "That's what I was trying to say on the river bank! You just frowned exactly like a homeless man we met in the Valley of High Hopes. His name was Horatio Banks. Are you related to him?"

"My name is Barb Banks," said Barb slowly. "And my grandpa's name was Horatio. He's been missing for years."

"There was a fight," said Nicola. "About chocolate."

"That's right," said Barb. "My mother says it was so

stupid. My grandpa slammed the front door and never came back. They looked for him for years."

"He thinks nobody has forgiven him yet," explained Shimlara. "He's just waiting in the valley for someone to go and find him."

"Oh! This is *incredible.* My grandmother will be excited! I'll have to go right now and tell her!" said Barb. She did Nicola's bandage back up and stood. "Thank you! The Banks family is greatly in your debt!"

She ran from the room, almost colliding with Sean, Tyler, and Greta, who were just about to open the door.

"You all right, Nic?" asked Sean.

That was probably the most affectionate thing Sean had ever said to her. It almost brought tears to Nicola's eyes.

"I'm fine," said Nicola. "What's that you've got there?"

Sean was holding a long rectangular-shaped package under his arm. "We saw the package waiting for you downstairs at reception when we were coming back," said Tyler.

"It's from Enrico," said Greta, pointing at a big red wax crest with Enrico's name on the bottom of the package.

On the front it said:

FOR THE ATTENTION OF: NICOLA BERRY

CARE OF THE WHY NOT DROP INN

Nicola felt her heart begin to thump.

Sean laid the package on the bed and they all looked at it with foreboding.

"I bet it's nothing nice," said Shimlara.

"But I guess I'd better open it, anyway," said Nicola, and she began to tear at the paper.

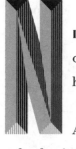

22

NICOLA DIDN'T MEAN TO SCREAM WHEN SHE REC-
ognized what was in the box. She just couldn't
help it.

At first she had thought it was an animal.
An animal with soft, shining brown hair. Maybe
a dead animal.

"What is it?" asked Sean.

And then Nicola recognized the distinctive brown
tinged with red color. It was the color of Katie's hair.

That's when she screamed.

"But what is it?" cried Shimlara. "I don't know what
it is!"

"It's Katie's hair," said Greta quietly. She reached into
the box and pulled out the long chunk of hair. "Enrico cut
off her hair so she's not a hairity any longer. He's made her
ordinary."

"But he hasn't hurt her, right?" said Tyler. Panic made
his voice skid in all directions.

"Didn't she say she was going to cut off her hair when
she got back to Earth?" said Shimlara.

"Yes," said Nicola, trying to calm herself down.

"She did say that. So hopefully she won't be too upset."

"There's a letter for you," said Sean, reaching into the box and pulling out a silver envelope. Breathing shallowly Nicola took the letter and opened it. She read out loud:

Dear Nicola,

It gives me great pleasure to enclose your friend's hair as a little something to remind you of your stupidity and selfishness. She has paid the ultimate sacrifice for YOUR mistakes and has indicated to me that she will never, ever forgive you for it. I do not blame her.

"Yeah right," interrupted Sean sarcastically. "Because Katie is such an unforgiving person."

Nicola continued reading:

In case you are even more stupid than I have realized, let me be quite clear on the nature of your mistakes.

Your first was to spread scandalous lies about me in the newspaper. I will NOT tolerate any form of bad publicity.

"Lies!" exploded Shimlara. "But it's all true!"

Your second mistake was revealing to one of my undercover thugs that you had no intention of fulfilling your mission.

```
I believe your exact words were, "Don't
worry, we would never hurt Topaz."
```

"Who was the undercover thug?" asked Sean. "Was it Horatio? I thought he looked sketchy."

"It wasn't Horatio. That's what Nicola said to that toothless man who sold us the Shock-Sticks," said Greta.

"But he had the little *t* on his forehead," protested Nicola. "I thought he was a Topaz supporter."

"It must have been fake," said Shimlara.

Nicola felt sick. It wasn't like making a mistake on a math test. It was a mistake that could cost her friend's life.

She continued reading:

```
Let me be clear, Nicola. I require the
Space Brigade to eliminate Topaz Silverbell.
If I do not receive evidence that this
task has been completed within the next
forty-eight hours, I shall cut off your
friend's food supply, followed by her water
supply, followed by her air supply. I am
extremely softhearted and it will pain me
to do this, but I am prepared to make these
sorts of sacrifices for my planet.
     I look forward to seeing this matter
reach a satisfactory conclusion ASAP. I'm
sure you don't want word getting out that
the Space Brigade is incapable of completing
the simplest mission.
```

My wife and children send their fondest regards.

Yours,

Enrico, Commander in Chief,

the Planet of Shobble

Nicola threw back the covers and climbed out of bed. Her legs felt wobbly and strange.

"We have to get out of here right now," she said. "We have to get to Topaz fast and get her help." Nicola imagined Katie starving, thirsty, and gasping for air. Nicola was so worried she felt like she was going crazy.

"Barb said you should be resting," said Shimlara. "Maybe you should stay here while we all go on and find Topaz."

Nicola gave her a blank stare until Shimlara held up her palms and said, "Just a suggestion. It's up to you."

"Where are the ShobGobbles?" snapped Nicola.

"They're in the inn's stables," answered Tyler.

"Right," said Nicola. "We'll meet at the stables in five minutes."

"Um—what should we do with Katie's hair?" asked Greta nervously, holding up the hair in one hand so it looked like someone's fancy dress wig. For a moment Nicola felt like she might burst into tears.

"Why don't I braid it?" asked Greta in the hopes of providing a good distraction. "That way it will be easier to carry without getting tangled and then Katie can keep it if she wants to."

Nicola nodded, unable to speak.

With deft fingers Greta turned the hair into a single, neat, chunky braid and presented it to Nicola. Nicola's eyes blurred. That was the way Katie wore it for gym.

Nicola took a shaky breath and carefully packed the braid into her backpack along with Enrico's venomous letter.

She looked up at the others and saw they were all watching her, their faces tense with worry. If she fell apart, they all might, and that wouldn't help Katie at all.

"I bet Katie looks *great* with short hair!" she said. "Anyway, what are you all just standing there for? I'll see you at the stables."

They all smiled with relief. Shimlara's voice came silently into her head: *You're the best, Nic.*

Thanks, Shimlara, replied Nicola without speaking. *Now please get out of my head!*

Everyone left and Nicola quickly began to get dressed. Her arm ached and she looked longingly back at the bed.

Downstairs a plump, smiling woman sat at reception. She put down a magazine she'd been reading called *The Shobble Woman's Daily* with pictures of beautiful women, all caressing their long, brown hair. "How are you? You look much better than when they brought you in last night."

"I'm much better, thank you," said Nicola.

"Well, I guess our great commander in chief must have had a very good reason for taking down all the protective glass on the Safe Hands Bridge," sighed the woman. "But it's terrible to see nice people like you with such awful wounds from the Biters."

Mmmmm. Nicola was pretty sure that Enrico didn't have a good reason at all.

"It's a pity you have to rush off so soon," said the woman. "We were excited to have guests from other planets staying with us. Where are you off to?"

The woman's face was so friendly, it was impossible to imagine her being a spy for Enrico, but this time Nicola wasn't taking any chances.

"We're on an important mission for the commander in chief," she said. "And we—umm—we're definitely going to do it! Absolutely! We sure are!"

Sean raised an eyebrow and Nicola remembered Silent Fred writing, "No need to overdo it, love," on the blackboard to Joy.

"Oh, well, that's good, dear," said the woman absentmindedly, before returning to her magazine.

Just then, the front door of the inn swung open and Tyler appeared from outside.

Sweat dripped from his forehead. "We've got a problem."

23

HE ShobGobbles were lying on their sides, snuggled into comfortable positions on the ground, and gently snoring.

"They won't wake up," said Shimlara despairingly. She was standing over her own ShobGobble with her hands on her hips. "No matter what we try."

Nicola knelt beside Quicksilver and yelled in his ear, *"Wake up!"* Quicksilver didn't even twitch.

"They're going to be asleep for at least a week," said Greta.

"What?" Nicola swung her head to look at her. "How do you know that?"

Greta silently handed her a single sheet of paper. It was pinned to the stable wall.

ATTENTION: SPACE BRIGADE

WE KNOW THE MISSION THAT ENRICO HAS SET FOR YOU. WE WILL DEFEND TOPAZ SILVERBELL WITH OUR LIVES! WE KINDLY SUGGEST YOU IGNORE HIS DASTARDLY REQUEST AND RETURN TO YOUR OWN PLANET. ALTERNATIVELY, FEEL FREE TO ENJOY A RELAXING CHOCOLATE

TASTING VACATION—WE WELCOME TOURISTS.
HOWEVER, IF YOU COME ANYWHERE NEAR
TOPAZ SILVERBELL THE CONSEQUENCES WILL
BE SERIOUS.

YOURS,
THE TOPAZ SUPPORTERS COMMITTEE

P.S. YOUR SHOBGOBBLES HAVE NOT BEEN
HARMED IN ANY WAY. THEY WILL SIMPLY
ENJOY A REFRESHING COMA FOR THE NEXT
SEVEN DAYS. WE DO APOLOGIZE FOR THE
INCONVENIENCE, BUT WE MUST DEFEND
OUR LEADER. IN SPITE OF THE LIES ENRICO
MIGHT HAVE TOLD YOU, TOPAZ IS TRYING
TO DO THE BEST THING FOR THE PEOPLE OF
SHOBBLE.

"Well, this is just great," said Sean. "Don't these stupid Topaz supporters know we're on their side? What are we supposed to do? The bad guys hate us and the good guys hate us, too!"

He turned away from them, his face red, his fists clenched. Suddenly, to Nicola's shock, he punched the stable wall so hard pieces of wood fell to the ground. Nicola had never seen him so angry.

"Ow!" said Sean miserably, and cradled his grazed knuckle in the other hand.

For some reason, Sean's anger made Nicola feel calm

and mature. Punching walls wasn't going to help the situation.

"We're just going to have to get to Topaz and explain what's happened," said Nicola.

"But how?" said Tyler. "It will take us forever to get to the Cloud-Capped Mountain on foot."

"I don't know," admitted Nicola.

They sat on the stable floor next to their snoring ShobGobbles. Sean sucked his knuckle and looked embarrassed.

Shimlara got up and walked over to a notice board filled with brochures that were obviously meant to appeal to visitors to the inn. They were advertising things like Biter-sighting trips on the Raging River and tours of a marshmallow mine.

"Hey!" said Shimlara. She snatched a leaflet off the board and held it out for them.

It said HOT-AIR BALLOON TRIPS TO THE CLOUD-CAPPED MOUNTAIN.

"Perfect!" said Nicola excitedly.

"No, it's not," said Greta. "Look what it says at the bottom."

"'Picnic lunch provided,'" read out Sean. "What's the problem with that?"

"Farther down."

"Oh," said everybody at the same time.

At the bottom of the brochure it said: BOOKINGS ACCEPTED FROM HAIRITIES ONLY.

"We'd be fine if we had Katie," said Shimlara.

"Katie isn't a hairity anymore," said Greta. "No more special treatment for her." She sounded far too pleased about it. Nicola wanted to slap her.

Shimlara dropped the brochure and slumped back on the ground again. Nobody said anything for a while. They all looked at the floor in front of them.

Finally Tyler lifted his head. "I might have an idea," he said slowly. "I don't know if it's stupid or not. It involves Shimlara."

"Go on," said Nicola.

Tyler's eyes were fixed on Shimlara. "Well, if Shimlara's hair was straight, wouldn't that make her a hairity?"

Everyone looked at Shimlara's dark brown, curly long hair.

"So what?" said Sean. "If my hair was long, I'd be a hairity, too."

"Well, what if we *made* Shimlara's hair straight?"

"How would we do that?"

Tyler didn't answer. He took off his glasses and polished them with the edge of his T-shirt. He put them back on and raised his eyebrows at them.

Everyone stared at him. Nicola wondered if he'd just lost his mind.

And then suddenly they all got it.

"Your mom's straightening iron!" everyone yelled at once.

24

I DON'T KNOW IF IT'S WORKING," WHISPERED SHIMlara to Nicola. "Nobody is taking any notice of me."

The Space Brigade walked down the main street of the village near the Why Not Drop Inn on their way to the hot-air balloon rental shop. Shimlara's hair was now dead straight, about a foot longer than when it was curly.

"Just wait," said Nicola.

At that moment a little girl walking nearby tugged at her mother's arm and pointed at Shimlara.

"Here we go," said Nicola. "Get ready to be famous."

The mother and her daughter came shyly over to Shimlara, their faces flushed with excitement.

"Excuse me," stammered the little girl to Shimlara. "Could I have your signograph? I think you're the most *beautiful* hairity I've ever seen."

"Of course," said Shimlara grandly. She flicked back her hair and signed the book with a flamboyant flourish.

"What's it like being a hairity?" asked the girl's mother.

"Well, I know it *seems* glamorous," said Shimlara, "but honestly, I'm just an ordinary, down-to-Globagaskar,

I mean down-to-Earth, I mean down-to-*Shobble* person like you."

"Oh!" The woman clasped her hands together as if she couldn't think of anything more wonderful than to be Shimlara.

As they walked off, Nicola noticed that Shimlara was already developing a different way of walking: a rather arrogant sort of saunter. As they continued on, there was a sudden blinding flash. "Shimlara! Shimlara! Over here!" An eager photographer was already dancing alongside them. He must have read the little girl's signograph book to get her name so quickly. It was extraordinary.

Shimlara tossed her hair over one shoulder, put one hand on her thrust-out hip, and posed for the photo.

"Gorgeous! Fabulous! You're wonderful!" cried the photographer and blew her a kiss. Shimlara blew one back.

Either Shimlara was an excellent actress, or being famous had gone straight to her head.

"Here's the balloon rental place," said Greta, who had been looking for the address on the brochure.

"Maybe I should go in on my own," said Shimlara.

"Good idea, your Highness," muttered Greta.

They all waited outside. A moment later Shimlara was back again, holding five tickets fanned out in her hand.

"No problemo," she said. "We leave in twenty minutes. We meet the balloon and the pilot down at the edge of the Sweet Dream Swamplands. Our pilot's name is Philippe."

"Did they mind taking non-hairities?" asked Nicola.

"They thought it was unusual," said Shimlara. "But I just acted like an eccentric celebrity. Actually, I could get used to this."

On the walk to the Swamplands they stopped by the Why Not Drop Inn to let everyone there know that the ShobGobbles would be staying for the week.

As the group walked on, Shimlara stopped every five minutes to sign another autograph or pose for a photograph. Her saunter became a swagger.

The others lagged behind.

"Look at the back of Shimlara's head," whispered Tyler. "The curls are coming back."

"It must be the humidity. At least that's what my mom says whenever her straightened hair begins to curl. Let's hope she doesn't have curly hair by the time we get to the balloon," said Nicola. "Or the pilot won't let us on."

"That would take her down a notch," muttered Greta.

"Speaking of the pilot," said Sean. "Don't you think it would be a good idea if we got rid of him?"

"What do you mean?" said Nicola nervously. "You don't mean kill him?"

"Yeah, and I've changed my name to Enrico," said Sean sarcastically. "*Of course not!* I mean maybe we should leave without him. Otherwise we'll have to convince him to wait around while we talk to Topaz. It might be useful to have the hot-air balloon to fly back to Enrico's mansion."

"So we'd be stealing it," said Nicola.

"No, we'd be borrowing it," said Sean. "Just for a little while. For an excellent cause."

"So how would we get rid of the pilot?"

"I don't know. We'd have to wait and see if there was an opportunity. Do you think you could fly it, Tyler?"

There was no question Tyler was the only one who would have a hope of flying a hot-air balloon.

Tyler adjusted his glasses nervously. "We took my sister on a hot-air balloon ride for her birthday," he said. "So I was asking the pilot lots of questions. Anyway, you can't actually steer a balloon. You only control whether the balloon goes up or down by adjusting the heat in the burner. So you have to find the layer of wind going where you want to go. I guess I could give it a try."

Nicola saw that Tyler had that same half-exhilarated, half-petrified expression on his face that he got when he flew a spaceship for the first time.

"Okay," said Nicola. "Well, *if* we get a chance I guess we should try and take off without him."

Shimlara called out, "The Swamplands are just ahead!" A group of eager fans was now trotting along beside her, hanging on to her every word.

They came to a soggy swamp that stretched as far as the eye could see. Nicola was glad that Quicksilver was sleeping peacefully. She wouldn't have liked making him trudge through all that mud.

"Look!" Tyler said. "They're about to inflate the balloon! That's the best part!"

Nicola could see a big brown wicker basket lying on its side and attached to a massive piece of shiny fabric that was obviously the balloon. As they got closer there was a *whoosh* sound and a flame burst alight in the basket.

"They've turned the burner on," explained Tyler. "They're going to fill the balloon with hot air."

"Because hot air rises, right?" asked Sean.

"Exactly."

Slowly the huge balloon began to puff out with air until it hovered above them, as tall as a building. The basket was held to the ground by a series of ropes and pegs.

A man with red hair and a matching mustache approached Shimlara. Nicola glanced over at Shimlara and saw more new curls popping up at the back of her head. None of her fans seemed to have noticed yet. They were too busy gazing at her with adoration.

"Shimlara, maybe you should wear your baseball cap," hissed Nicola. "So you don't get sunburned."

"Oh, I like a little sun," said Shimlara.

"No, I *really* think you should," said Nicola meaningfully.

Shimlara blinked. She was obviously reading Nicola's mind. "Oh yes! Good idea!" She grabbed her cap from her backpack and put it on, so all you could see were smooth tresses falling over her shoulder.

The redhaired man came up to Shimlara and bowed low. As he spoke he lovingly caressed his mustache as if it were a precious little pet. "I am Philippe. It will be my pleasure to be your pilot for today. They've forecast a minor hurricane so it might be a bit bumpy at times, but don't worry—I have plenty of experience. Now, I believe you also have some guests?" He looked around for the guests as if the rest of the Space Brigade were invisible.

"Yes," said Shimlara. "These are my friends, Nicola, Sean, Tyler, and Greta."

"*These* are your *friends*?" said Philippe disbelievingly. Then he smiled as if he'd worked it out. "So you're a charity worker! How inspiring! Well, if you and your 'friends' would like to climb aboard, we'll be off in a jiffy."

He helped Shimlara climb into the basket, holding on to her elbow as if she were a delicate old lady.

"How are we going to get rid of him?" whispered Sean as they crowded in behind Shimlara. Not surprisingly, Philippe didn't bother to help the non-hairities.

"I've got an idea," Shimlara whispered back. She grabbed her ear and looked panic-stricken. "Oh no! I've lost a very expensive, irreplaceable diamond earring. Philippe, will you see if I've dropped it on the ground over there?"

Philippe had been just about to climb into the basket with them.

"Of course," he said immediately.

"I think I dropped it way, *way* over there." Shimlara pointed vaguely into the distance.

"No problem," said Philippe.

"Hey!" someone in the crowd called out. "What's happening to the hairity's hair?"

Nicola saw that curls and tendrils were springing up all over Shimlara's hair. The heat from the balloon must have been making her sweat. And sweat, Nicola knew from her mother, was the enemy of straightened hair.

"She's not a hairity at all!" someone else called out. "She's a fake! Her hair is *curly*."

Philippe turned back to look at Shimlara. He froze on the spot when he saw Shimlara's hair.

"Time to get out of here!" said Sean, and he produced the big bread knife he'd brought from home and lunged for the ropes that were keeping them tethered to the ground.

Philippe's face turned tomato-red. *"I knew there was something not right about you! You're just a lot of dirty commoners! Get out of my balloon now!"*

Tyler was bent over the balloon's burner muttering urgently to himself.

Philippe came running back and grabbed for the edge of the basket. Sean used the knife to slice through another rope and the balloon lurched sideways. Philippe tried again, this time managing to latch onto the side of the basket.

"Excuse me, we are *not* dirty commoners!" screamed Greta (although she didn't sound exactly *ladylike*). She took off her shoe and used it to bang hard at Philippe's fingers.

"Ow!" Philippe released his hand and toppled to the ground just as Sean cut the final rope.

At the same time Tyler said, "Aha!" and turned a control on the burner. There was a hiss and a burst of hot air.

The hot-air balloon floated straight up into the sky.

25

HERE WAS NO SOUND AT ALL.

They were floating silently through the arch of a rainbow. It was like flying through a tunnel of shimmering color. The fabric of the balloon fluttered gently in the breeze. The basket swayed softly. No one said a word.

Nicola felt her shoulders sag. There was something about the sudden unexpected silence that was extremely relaxing. She looked at all her friends and the rich colors flickering across their faces. If only Katie were here, this would be one of those perfect memories that Nicola could store away in her mind ready to pull out next time she was stuck in a boring math lesson.

Beneath them Philippe and Shimlara's angry fans ran around in circles like furious ants.

Shimlara removed her cap. Her hair blew wild and curly in the breeze. Everyone smiled when they saw it and Shimlara chuckled. "Guess I'm just a dirty commoner like the rest of you."

"Did you like being a hairity?" asked Nicola curiously. It was a relief to see Shimlara looking like herself again.

"It was weird," said Shimlara. "It sort of went to my head in the beginning. I thought I really *was* amazing just because everyone was treating me that way."

"It went to your head, did it?" said Sean innocently. "Wow. You couldn't tell at all."

"Okay, okay, I know I went overboard. But even though I sort of loved it, it made me feel kind of lonely, too. I missed being me."

"We missed you being you, too," said Tyler.

He licked his finger and held it outside the balloon.

"What are you doing?" asked Greta.

"I'm checking which way the wind is blowing."

"So how does licking your finger tell you that?"

"I don't know," admitted Tyler. "My dad does it before he puts up the beach umbrella. It seemed like the right thing to do." He adjusted the burner slightly and peered out over the edge of the basket. "Anyway, it looks like we're heading in the right direction at the moment. Look. That's the Cloud-Capped Mountain."

He pointed toward the dramatic outline of a craggy mountain silhouetted crisply against a bright blue sky.

Nicola said, "We're lucky with the weather. It's a beautiful day."

"Yes." Shimlara squinted thoughtfully up at the blue sky. "Although don't forget what Philippe said."

Nicola had forgotten. "What did he say?"

"Hey!" At that moment a gust of cold air blew Greta's hat straight off her head and whipped it away.

Nicola watched the cap being whirled this way and that and suddenly she remembered all too clearly what Philippe had said:

. . . they're forecasting a minor hurricane . . .

She said cheerily, "At least they aren't forecasting a *major—*" She gulped on the word *hurricane* as another gust of wind rocked the balloon and knocked her hard against Greta.

"Watch it," said Greta automatically, but she, like the rest of the Space Brigade, was frowning up at the huge banks of heavy gray clouds rolling rapidly across the sky like ocean waves. There was a deep rumble of thunder and a sudden spatter of icy rain against the fabric of the balloon.

"This doesn't look good," said Tyler. There were specks of water on his glasses. He brushed them away impatiently.

"It's gotten extra cold." Shimlara shivered and wrapped her arms around herself. Directly above them was a patch of bright blue sky like a leftover piece of a completely different day.

"How are we going to fly this through a hurricane? We

shouldn't have left Philippe behind," said Greta crossly, as if she hadn't been bashing his knuckles with her shoe just five minutes ago.

"All we've got to do is stay in the eye of the hurricane," said Sean. "I saw it in a movie. That's where you're safe."

"Oh, is that all? Well then we shouldn't have a problem!" Tyler didn't normally sound irritable and sarcastic. *He must be frightened*, thought Nicola.

They were in a hot-air balloon with a hurricane about to start. It really didn't get much worse than this. For some reason, instead of crying, Nicola started to laugh.

"What's so funny?" snapped Greta. "This isn't funny! There is nothing funny about this at all!"

That only made Nicola laugh harder.

"Is she hysterical?" asked Shimlara. "Nicola, are you hysterical?"

Nicola decided to pull herself together before everyone started enthusiastically slapping her across the face.

"I'm not hysterical," she said and tried to think of something leaderish and sensible to say. A notice stuck to the inside of the basket caught her eye.

"Now will everyone just calm down and take a look at this notice," she said bossily, as if everyone else had been the ones falling about, laughing. They all crouched down to read.

INSTRUCTIONS FOR WHAT TO DO IN THE CASE OF A MINOR OR MAJOR HURRICANE

IN THE CASE OF A MINOR HURRICANE . . .

YOUR CHANCES OF SURVIVAL ARE APPROXIMATELY 48.5–63.5 PERCENT. WE RECOMMEND THAT YOU:

1. PLACE AN INFLATABLE BUBBLE-JACKET (STORED UNDER THE BURNER) OVER YOUR HEAD AND TIE THE STRAPS AROUND YOUR WAIST AS PER THE DIAGRAM. BUBBLE-JACKETS ARE DESIGNED TO INFLATE ON IMPACT WITH A HARD SURFACE. IN THIS EVENT YOU WILL FIND YOURSELF ENCASED WITHIN A BOUNCY RUBBER BALL FOR YOUR OWN SAFETY. UNFORTUNATELY IT IS NOT POSSIBLE TO REMOVE YOURSELF FROM THE BALL WITHOUT ASSISTANCE. WE APOLOGIZE FOR ANY INCONVENIENCE.

2. SIT ON THE FLOOR OF THE BASKET.

3. IF YOU ARE ACCOMPANIED BY ACQUAINTANCES OR LOVED ONES IT MIGHT BE A GOOD IDEA TO CONFIRM YOUR FEELINGS, E.G. "I LOVE YOU," "I AM QUITE FOND OF YOU," OR "I HAVE NEVER REALLY LIKED YOU ALL THAT MUCH," AS THE CASE MAY BE. YOU MAY ALSO WANT TO ASK FOR FORGIVENESS FOR PREVIOUS WRONGS, E.G. HURTFUL COMMENTS, FORGOTTEN BIRTHDAYS, ETC.

*NOTE—DO NOT ATTEMPT TO FLY THE BALLOON TO ANY SPECIFIC LOCATION. THIS IS A HURRICANE, FOLKS. THE BALLOON IS GOING TO DO WHATEVER THE HURRICANE WANTS. THE BEST YOU CAN HOPE FOR IS THAT YOU'LL BE SLAMMED GENTLY INTO THE NEAREST MOUNTAIN. BY THE WAY, THERE

WILL ALWAYS BE SOME JOKER IN THE PACK WHO SUGGESTS
HEADING FOR THE EYE OF THE STORM. THIS IS LIKE ADVISING
A BANKRUPT PERSON TO TRY AND WIN THE LOTTERY. SURE, IT
WOULD BE *GREAT*, BUT WHAT ARE THE ODDS? (TEENY-WEENY.)

IN THE CASE OF A MAJOR HURRICANE . . .

YOUR CHANCES OF SURVIVAL ARE APPROXIMATELY 0 PERCENT.
WE RECOMMEND:

ENJOY YOUR LAST FEW MOMENTS OF LIFE!

THANK YOU FOR FLYING WITH SHOBBLE'S LEADING HOT-AIR
BALLOONISTS.

Nicola was the fastest reader, so she finished first. Her
earlier laughter had vanished, although she could still feel
the giggly sensation at the back of her throat. She watched
the emotions fly across everyone's faces as they read. They
frowned, they chewed their lips, and they went bright red
or ghost-white.

One by one, as each person finished reading the sign,
they'd turn their head toward Nicola in search of guidance.

26

PHILIPPE DID SAY A *MINOR* HURRICANE, DIDN'T he?" Shimlara gripped the side of the basket as it rocked violently. Long strands of her hair whipped across her face and caught in her mouth. "Not a major hurricane? Tell me he didn't say major!"

"He definitely said minor." Tyler squinted up at the mass of angry black clouds that was gathering above them. "Although this looks pretty major to me."

"I don't see what's so bad about suggesting that you try to fly to the eye of the storm." Sean looked offended by the notice. "It makes perfect sense!"

"I *knew* taking the hot-air balloon was a bad idea." Greta pulled out a Honeyville Primary raincoat from her backpack, her lips pursed, as if someone had purposely arranged the hurricane just to annoy her.

"Well, it's funny you never mentioned it," said Shimlara.

"I knew there was no point. Nobody ever listens to me."

Suddenly it was pouring fat, heavy raindrops. Within seconds everyone was drenched and shivering uncontrollably. Nicola felt icy raindrops running down the back of her clothes. Thunder boomed and lightning cracked like a whip, illuminating their wet, frightened faces. The basket rocked so hard everyone clumsily lurched about trying to keep balance. Shimlara's elbow collided with Greta's nose.

"Ow!"

"It's not my fault!"

Nicola imagined how their hot-air balloon must have looked from the ground. Probably like a helpless butterfly being tossed about the huge backdrop of the sky. Philippe was no doubt laughing his head off at their predicament. Would they survive? And what would happen to Katie if the rest of them were killed in a ballooning accident?

Tyler yelled over the noise of the rain, "We've got to put our bubble-jackets on like the notice says!"

Sean crouched down and pulled out red jackets from a box beneath the balloon's burner. He handed one to each person. They looked like puffier versions of ordinary life jackets. Nicola took ages to work hers out. Finally she managed to pull it over her head and tie the straps around her waist.

"So now we've all got to sit down!" she cried. She looked around and saw that she'd taken so long, the others were already all crouching around the edges of the basket with their heads bowed against the rain and the wind.

She wedged herself between Greta and Sean.

Greta leaned over and spoke into Nicola's ear. "I've always found you pretty annoying, Nicola."

"What?" Nicola wasn't sure if she'd heard right.

"You know, the notice said to tell people how you really feel."

Nicola couldn't respond because suddenly the wind got so strong it was difficult to breathe. The basket jerked back and forth, swooped up in an arc, plummeted down, and then soared back up again. Without thinking, Nicola reached for Sean's and Greta's hands. Both of them latched on and held on for dear life. Nicola looked up briefly and saw that all the Space Brigade were holding hands, their foreheads pressed against their knees, a huddled, terrified, sodden circle on the floor of the basket. Nicola pressed her face back down against her knees as well.

The howling of the wind sounded horrible. A *whooooo-hooooo-ooooo* sound like a ghost screaming.

Or was it Shimlara screaming?

Or was it herself screaming?

Or was it *all of them* screaming?

The balloon turned into a merry-go-round on fast-forward. Around and around it went, faster and faster. Then Nicola opened her eyes and saw the side of a mountain looming impossibly high above them like the side of a ship.

She heard Sean say, "Oh no. Oh no. Oh no," but before she could react, both his and Greta's hands were torn from her grasp. Suddenly, the basket flipped upside down. The Space Brigade came tumbling out like marbles from a jar, plummeting thousands of feet through the air.

27

THIS TIME NICOLA WASN'T GOING TO LAND IN AN icy river. This time she was going to land face-first on that icy, snow-covered mountain rushing up to meet her. This time there was no way she could survive (and by the way, how *dare* Greta say she was annoying? Now she would never have the chance to answer her back!). This time her nose was probably going to be smashed to smithereens, which would presumably be *extremely* painful. This time—

Kerpow!

Before any part of Nicola actually hit the ground, something exploded all around her. Something huge and rubbery and damp-smelling.

She held her breath, waiting for the terrible pain.

Which part of her was hurt or broken?

No part, as far as she could tell.

She was fine. She was alive.

I just survived a fall from a hot-air balloon.

Nicola took a shaky breath.

I just survived a fall from a hot-air balloon! It was unbelievable.

Her whole face had been scrunched up tight in preparation for hitting the ground. Slowly, carefully, she unscrunched it and opened her eyes.

Her bubble-jacket had been transformed into a gigantic round rubber ball from which only her head protruded like a tortoise. The ball was rolling backward and forward on the spot. She tried to move her arms and legs and found that she was trapped within the ball, exactly as the notice had said. Well, she couldn't complain. The bubble-jacket had done its job and saved her life.

She looked up and saw she'd landed underneath some sort of rocky ledge that protected her from the hurricane. She could hear the wind still howling and the rain pounding. She wondered where the others had landed. Were they all safe? Had all their bubble-jackets worked? She hoped Shimlara had put hers on properly. Sometimes she could be a bit haphazard with that sort of thing.

Nicola's nose was itchy and because her arms were trapped she couldn't scratch it. She tried to drop her face forward to rub it on the edge of the ball, but she couldn't bend her neck far enough.

Well, it was only an itchy nose. She could cope with an itchy nose.

Oh, but this was *unbearable*.

She twitched her nose and shook her head.

It was *excruciating*. It was worse than the Biter wound on her arm (which was now aching again thanks to all the smashing about in the hot-air balloon). If she didn't scratch her nose within the next five seconds she would *explode*.

Her rubber ball rolled forward. Nicola glanced down and forgot all about her itchy nose.

Oh . . . my . . . goodness.

The ball rolled back again and Nicola wondered if she'd imagined what she'd just seen. She wished her hands were free so she could rub her eyes. She blinked and shook her head to clear it. Surely not. It couldn't be possible. She could not be that unlucky.

The ball rolled forward again.

Nicola looked down. She heard herself make a strange squeaky sound like a mouse being suffocated.

She hadn't imagined it.

She had landed on a rocky shelf on the side of the Cloud-Capped Mountain. Directly beneath her was a *view*.

In fact it was quite an impressive view of the planet of Shobble. She could see oceans and mountains and tiny dollhouse-sized villages. But views should be enjoyed from safe, comfy spots: like a window seat in an airplane, or while eating dinner in a revolving restaurant, or taking photos from the top of the Eiffel Tower. Nicola could think of a million more suitable ways to enjoy a view rather than being encased in a huge plastic ball that kept rolling to a stop inches away from the side of a mountaintop.

"Nicola! You're on the edge of a *cliff*!"

It was Sean's voice. Nicola was filled with relief. At the same time she was a bit irritated. Talk about stating the obvious.

She craned her neck with difficulty in the direction of his voice and saw that Greta, Tyler, and Sean had all landed close together under a clump of trees a safe distance back from the cliff, but there was no sign of Shimlara. The rest of their bubble-jackets had inflated. It was a strange sight seeing them bobbing about with only their heads poking out of the huge red balls.

Nicola's ball rolled back under the ledge. Safe.

Then it rolled forward again. Not safe. Not safe at all.

Safe. Not safe. Safe. Not safe.

Each time the ball teetered on the edge of the cliff Nicola held her breath. Then she let it out in a whoosh each time it rolled back under the ledge. She was starting to feel dizzy. Could this go on forever?

"Don't worry, Nicola! We're working on a solution!" Tyler's voice came faintly across the mountain.

Well, that was comforting. Maybe they'd worked out a way to get themselves out of their bubble-jackets.

"Actually, we've got *no idea* what to do!" That was Greta.

Nicola could just imagine what was happening now. Sean and Tyler were saying, "Why did you say that?" and Greta was looking put-out and saying something like, "Well, I don't see any point in giving her false hope."

Safe. Not safe. Safe. Not safe.

"You may as well just give up."

I know. It's not like anyone is just going to turn up. I mean, who would take a stroll in a hurricane?

"It's all over. Just accept it."

Well, that's maybe a bit over*dramatic.*

"Achoo!"

"Bless you!"

Nicola realized with a start that she hadn't actually been having that rather depressing conversation in her own head. There was a real person somewhere nearby!

She twisted her head around in the direction of the voice. It was a girl speaking. A girl with a stuffed-up nose. "All that work has been for nothing. *Nothing!* Achoo! I may as well have just stayed in bed! Achoo! Everything is just pointless and stupid and I can't stop sneezing! Achoo! Achoo! Achoo!"

Finally Nicola saw her just over her left shoulder. Obviously this girl wasn't afraid of heights because she was sitting right on the edge of the cliff, her legs dangling, sneezing into a huge hanky. She was wearing only a plain sleeveless tunic that left her thin white arms and legs bare. Her head was uncovered and her hair was a soaking wet mess. It made Nicola shiver just looking at her. She found herself thinking in her mother's voice, *For heaven's sakes! You're going to catch pneumonia dressed like that!*

"Um, excuse me?" Nicola called out.

The girl blew her nose hard and continued talking angrily to herself. "I may as well just move off this stupid planet and find somewhere else to live. I'll go spend a year backpacking around Earth! Achoo! I may as well. Nobody—achoo!—appreciates—achoo!—me, anyway!"

Nicola's ball rolled forward again and this time it seemed like it would roll over for sure. Could her bubble-jacket protect her twice? It seemed unlikely. She started to panic.

"Excuse me! I think I really need your help out of this thing!"

The girl suddenly looked up.

"Oh!" she said. "I didn't see you there. Sorry. Did you come over on one of those hot-air balloons? They've really got to stop flying during hurricanes."

She blew her nose one more time and stood up. "Here. Let me help you."

As she walked toward Nicola she gave her a friendly sort of grimace. "I guess you're not having a great day, either."

"Not really," admitted Nicola.

The girl had that characteristic rosy Shobble-person face—snub, freckled nose, and round blue eyes. And there was something else that was familiar about her. It couldn't be *her*, could it? After all this time? Standing right here in front of her, shivering and sniffing?

"I'm Topaz," said the girl. "Topaz Silverbell."

28

OPAZ LOOKED AT NICOLA EXPECTANTLY, WAITING
for her to introduce herself.

"Well, hi there!" said Nicola brightly. "Am I
glad to see *you*! At first I thought I was talking to
myself!"

Oh dear, Nicola thought, *I'm babbling.* She was trying
to distract Topaz because if Topaz thought that Nicola had
been sent to kill her, wasn't there a chance she might just
push her off the cliff as soon as she said the name Nicola?
After all, it would only take the tiniest shove.

Topaz raised an eyebrow. "And you are . . . ?"

"I'm, er, I'm . . ." The obvious thing to do would be to
make up a name, but for some reason the only name Nicola
could think of was Nicola.

"I'm Ni—Ni—um—Nilly!"

"Nilly?" frowned Topaz.

"Nilly," repeated Nicola miserably. A million names
now flooded her head. *Anne. Sara. Louise. Diane.* And all
she could come up with was *Nilly*.

Topaz sniffed loudly. She took her handkerchief from
her tunic pocket and blew her nose again.

"You're that Earthling, aren't you? Your name isn't Nilly. It's Nicola. Nicola Berry."

"Yes," agreed Nicola. "But—"

"You're the head of the Space Brigade. Enrico hired you to kill me."

"Yes, but—"

"Well, go ahead."

"Go ahead?"

"Go ahead and kill me." Topaz sneezed again and wrapped her arms around herself. "I was just thinking that someone might as well bump me off. So go ahead. Do your job. I won't even try and defend myself."

"Oh, but Topaz!" Nicola remembered the photo she'd seen in Enrico's file. Topaz had seemed so full of passion and life. Now she seemed sick and miserable, her eyes flat, her voice bitter.

"Come on! What are you waiting for?"

"Topaz, I don't want—"

"Hurry up! Get it over with! I'm not afraid!" Topaz lifted her chin and closed her eyes.

Nicola almost laughed. She said, "Well, it's actually a bit hard to kill you when I'm trapped in this ball."

"Oh." Topaz opened her eyes. "But don't you have special Earthling powers? Can't you shoot laser beams out of your eyes or something?" She almost seemed disappointed.

Nicola said, "I don't have any special powers and actually, if you don't help me out of this thing soon, I might die first."

All the time they'd been talking her ball had continued rolling back and forth. Now it was hovering once again on the edge of the cliff. Nicola gritted her teeth.

"Oh, right." Topaz sneezed again and sighed. "Okay, I'll help you out of there and *then* you can kill me, although I have to say, it hardly seems fair that I have to do my killer a favor, but then again, there isn't much *justice* on this planet, is there? Oh no, not unless your name is *Enrico*, of course, then it's a different story, then you get plenty of justice, and plenty of gold coins in your treasure account, too, while the rest of us have *zero* treasure account balances. Achoo! But that's no problem, we don't mind living in poverty, and why try and change things, because that's just the way it is, and, anyway, if Enrico catches you complaining he'll just arrange for your tongue to be burned so you can never speak again, oh, but we all pretend that sort of thing doesn't happen, don't we, let's all keep drilling and mining while the hairities get richer and we get poorer!"

All the time she was talking Topaz was rummaging through her pockets pulling out and discarding an array of different objects: crumpled up leaflets, tissues, a half-eaten

ShobbleChoc bar, a hair band, a paper clip, a transistor radio, and finally—a pin.

"This ought to do the trick," she said, and jabbed the pin into the rubber ball encasing Nicola.

There was a loud bang like a balloon bursting and a hiss of air.

Nicola found herself standing on firm ground, covered in shredded plastic.

"I've never understood why they don't just supply a pin with every bubble-jacket," said Topaz. "I bet it was designed by some stupid hairity. Okay, now are you ready to kill me? Hurry up, because I'm actually starting to change my mind. I might fight back. You don't look that scary."

Nicola stepped away from the side of the cliff and back under the ledge. The rain was becoming softer and the wind had stopped howling. It seemed like the hurricane had just about blown itself out.

Desperate for Topaz to see that they were friends, not enemies, Nicola began to speak in a rush. "We're not here to hurt you, Topaz. We're sympathetic to your cause! Enrico is holding our friend hostage. His plan was to get us to 'eliminate' you and then keep all of us prisoners in a glass cage, so everybody will think he's the good guy. All we want is to help you overthrow Enrico."

Topaz didn't say anything for a few seconds. Then she

sighed and looked away. "Well, *I* can't help you. I can't do anything. I'm giving up the cause. I don't care anymore. Enrico can do what he wants. I'm sorry about your friend, but there's nothing I can do."

Nicola's heart was sinking fast. Had they come all this way for *nothing*?

"But why are you giving up? What's wrong? Is it just because you've got a cold? Everything always feels worse when you're sick."

"No, it's more than that. It's—"

"Hey! Are you girls just going to sit around and chat all day? Maybe you could get your new friend to come and help us out, too, Nic! Greta needs to go to the bathroom!"

It was Sean hollering from across the mountain. Nicola felt mortified. Topaz was going to lose all respect for the Space Brigade. She could hear Greta yelling back at him, "Hey! That was *private* information!"

"Is that the rest of the Space Brigade?" Topaz looked amused in spite of herself.

"Yes," said Nicola. "That was my brother. I guess I should go and let them out." Suddenly she remembered Shimlara. "Oh—and another friend of ours was with us in the hot-air balloon! I need to find out where she landed. I hope her bubble-jacket inflated okay."

She felt as if she'd been neglecting Shimlara by not worrying about her for the last few minutes.

"Don't worry, I'll get my friends to form a search party," said Topaz. She pulled out what looked like some sort of transistor radio from her pocket and flicked a switch. "Topaz to Joshua. Topaz to Joshua. Come in, Joshua."

Immediately, a young boy's voice crackled forth from the radio. "Yeah, Joshua to Topaz, where have you *been*? Everyone has been worried about you. I just got a message from Mom saying if you weren't resting, she was coming up the mountain to put you to bed herself. I didn't mention that you were curing your cold by going for a walk in a hurricane!"

Topaz said, "Joshua, I'm fifteen years old."

"Why are you talking in your trying-to-sound-cool voice? Is someone there with you?"

Now it was Topaz's turn to look embarrassed.

"Brothers." Nicola rolled her eyes sympathetically.

Topaz said, "I'm here with Nicola Berry."

Joshua's voice changed. "The evil Earthling? Where are you? We're on our way!"

"It's okay, Joshua." Topaz smiled up at Nicola. "She's not that bad. In fact, she's actually pretty nice for an evil Earthling."

29

HERE SHE IS! OVER THERE!"

It was Topaz's brother, Joshua, who finally spotted Shimlara. Joshua was a short, square-shaped boy who brimmed with so much energy you couldn't imagine him standing still. He and Sean had quickly figured out that they were kindred spirits. As they'd run through the snow calling out Shimlara's name, Sean had been showing Joshua karate moves, while Joshua demonstrated a Shobble sport called Head Crunch. It seemed to involve running as fast as you could toward a particular spot in the snow and then diving in headfirst while yelling *"Head Crunch!"* Sean thought Head Crunch was hilarious and Joshua thought karate was hilarious, and they had both become sweaty and elated.

"Am I glad to see you!" shouted Shimlara when she saw them. *"I don't think I could take much more of this!"*

Nicola thought landing on the edge of a cliff had probably won her first prize for Worst Possible Place to Land in Your Bubble-Jacket but Shimlara had won second prize. She'd fallen right into the middle of a frozen lake. The good news was that her bubble-jacket had inflated properly and saved her from crashing through the ice. The bad news was that she was now trapped in a ball that turned on its own axis like a spinning coin. Shimlara's face was green.

"It was fun at first!" she cried. *"But now not so much!"*

Nicola went to run to her out on the lake, but Topaz stopped her. "Your shoes aren't convertible, are they?"

"Convertible?"

"It's a Shobble innovation for skating on our frozen seas." Topaz reached down and adjusted something on her shoes. Blades sprang out from the bottom.

"Don't worry, I'll get her." Topaz glided off smoothly across the ice toward the spinning Shimlara.

The rain had stopped, the sun was shining, and Shobble's rainbows were once again shimmering above them. The air on top of the Cloud-Capped Mountain was so pure, you wanted to drink it up in big refreshing gulps.

"Head-Crunch championships start now!" shouted Joshua.

"Yeah!" yelled Sean.

"Yeah!" yelled out Tyler, although not quite as enthusiastically. Nicola hoped he didn't smash his glasses trying to impress the other boys.

"I bet I can beat all of you with my gymnastics skills," said Greta.

"I've never heard of gymnastics skills, but give it your best shot, Earthling!" Joshua shouted.

Nicola was left standing on the side of the lake next to a tall, frizzy-haired girl who had joined them on the hunt for Shimlara. Topaz had introduced her as Serena Goldust. Serena seemed to be a quiet, serious girl with a soothing sort of stillness to her that was in marked contrast to both Joshua and Topaz.

As they watched Topaz skating across to Shimlara, Nicola said, "I hope you don't mind me asking, but is Topaz okay? She seems sort of depressed."

Serena kept her eyes fixed on Topaz and didn't say anything for a few seconds. Then she sighed. "Yes, she is depressed. It's partly because she's got a bad cold but other things have been getting her down. People keep telling her it's not worth fighting Enrico and that we're only making things worse for the people. They'd rather spend their lives reading about what the hairities eat for breakfast. Also, one of the marshmallow miners had an accident and it was our fault. We all felt terrible about that."

"What happened?" asked Nicola.

"Well, we broke into one of the marshmallow mines and exploded a fizz-bang bomb. They're *perfectly* safe. It's just a lot of noise and red smoke."

"I think we saw that," said Nicola, remembering the

explosion at the marshmallow mine when they'd first arrived on Shobble.

"We just wanted to hold up production a bit. We left behind a big sign saying, MARSHMALLOW MINERS SHOULD BE PAID FOR THEIR WORK. It all went really well except that two miners who were blinded by the smoke collided and broke their noses. Topaz's mother said that someone is always going to get hurt if we keep doing that sort of thing, but how else do we get noticed? And then we heard that Enrico had arranged for some Earthlings to try and kill us—well, that's when Topaz started saying we might as well give it all up."

"But Enrico shouldn't be allowed to get away with it!" said Nicola.

"I know," said Serena. "But what can we do? My father drilled for chocolate for over forty years. He worked on the most dangerous chocolate rigs where they drill for the rarest, sweetest chocolate at the bottom of the sea. His teeth have rotted from breathing in pure chocolate fumes every day of his life. And he has never been paid a single gold coin. Do you know how much they charge for ShobbleChoc in far-off galaxies? The profits are huge. And my dad just says, oh well, the hairities know best! I say, Dad, having long brown hair does not mean you've got a brain, it just means you've got long brown hair, and he says, yes,

Serena darling, whatever you say, and that's the end of that."

Nicola watched Topaz skate up to Shimlara and pop her bubble-jacket. Shimlara staggered and Topaz caught her. They talked for a few seconds and Nicola saw Shimlara's face light up with joy.

"Nic, it's *Topaz*!" called out Shimlara, as if Nicola hadn't figured this out already. "We've found Topaz!"

"I know!" called back Nicola.

But it seemed finding Topaz wasn't the answer to their problems at all.

3 0

ELCOME TO HEADQUARTERS," SNIFFED Topaz. "Not that it's going to be head-quarters for much longer."

The Space Brigade, Topaz, Joshua, and Serena were standing in front of a large boulder on the side of the mountain. Topaz kicked at something in the snow beneath her feet and the boulder slid back to reveal an enormous cave. Once the boulder was back over, you would never know the cave even existed.

There was a long table in the middle of the cave scattered with pens, newspaper clippings, and pieces of strange-looking equipment. Old placards were lined up against the walls of the cave with slogans like: THE TROUBLE WITH SHOBBLE IS ENRICO!; A HAIRITY WHO CARES IS A RARITY!; SHARE SHOBBLE'S PROFITS WITH THE PEOPLE!

There were three cots lined up against the walls where Topaz, Joshua, and Serena obviously slept. There was also a small stove and a basket full of food and supplies. It was clearly a place where people worked hard.

Topaz made her way straight to one of the beds. Her face was flushed. "Sorry, but I'm going to bed," she said.

"I think I've got a temperature." She got in and pulled the blankets over her shoulder and faced the wall. Joshua and Serena raised their eyebrows at each other.

"She'll bounce back to her old self as soon as her cold goes away," said Joshua. "She's not serious about giving up the cause."

"I am so serious," said Topaz, without turning her head from the wall.

"Of course you are," said Joshua, while silently shaking his head and mouthing "no, she's not" at the others.

"I am," said Topaz. Her voice began to drift off. "I've—had—just—about—enough." Seconds later, she was snoring.

"A nice long sleep will do her a world of good," said Nicola. Oh, why did her mother's words keep coming out of her mouth like that!

Luckily, before Sean could tease her mercilessly, Joshua mentioned food and distracted him.

"I've made some hizza," he said. "Who wants some?"

"What's hizza?" asked Sean suspiciously.

It turned out that *hizza* on Shobble was exactly the same as pizza on Earth—and it was fantastic, with a thin flaky crust, a thick, tasty topping, and lots of melted cheese.

"This is *p*izza, dude," said Sean, taking his fifth piece. "And it's very good."

"It's *h*izza," said Joshua. "And I know it's good. I'm going to be a chef one day—once we've overthrown Enrico."

"Well, I don't mean to be negative," said Greta. (*Here we go,* thought Nicola.) "But how are you ever going to overthrow Enrico when your leader has given up and gone to bed? We've come all this way to find you so we could work together to fight Enrico and so far, it's been a big waste of time."

"Greta," said Tyler, "if it wasn't for Topaz we'd still be stuck in our bubble-jackets."

"Well, if it wasn't for Topaz we wouldn't have been here in the first place. And meanwhile Katie is stuck in Enrico's clutches and we're all just sitting here on the other side of the planet eating *hizza*!"

Nicola had to admit she had a point.

"Hey, we didn't *ask* you to come here," said Joshua, starting to look angry. "We did our best to stop you when we arranged for your ShobGobbles to be put to sleep."

"Speaking of which, I hope that didn't hurt our lovely ShobGobbles," said Shimlara. "That was a pretty mean thing to do to poor, defenseless animals!"

"It's perfectly safe, and, anyway, we thought you were coming to kill my sister!" Joshua slammed his fist on the table. "We thought you were scary creatures from another planet!"

"Oh, we can be scary," said Sean, looking fierce, although the blob of tomato sauce on his nose spoiled the effect.

"Who is Katie?" interrupted Serena.

Nicola explained the whole story to Serena and Joshua. When she'd finished, Serena and Joshua were shaking their heads.

"Every time I think Enrico couldn't get anymore evil, he does," said Joshua. "And you say he's planning to burn all your tongues like he did to Silent Fred? How did you find that out?"

"I read his mind," explained Shimlara. "I'm from Globagaskar. We can read minds there."

"Oh, sure!" said Joshua. "So you can read minds? What am I thinking right now?"

He crossed his arms and closed his eyes.

Shimlara looked at him and Nicola saw her cheeks go pink.

"You're, ummm—"

"I knew you couldn't do it!"

Shimlara looked down at her lap with a little half-smile. She said, "You're wondering if all the girls on Globagaskar are as pretty as me."

Sean guffawed and Joshua's face turned scarlet. "How did you do that? Don't do that again! I won't be able to think anything private!"

"I only read your mind because you asked me to!" said Shimlara. "I won't do it again. It's bad manners to read people's minds." Nicola had never seen her look so flustered.

"So, *anyway*," said Nicola, deciding it was a good time to change the subject. "On our way here we met an interesting old man named Horatio. He told us about a clause in Shobble's constitution that says if you get enough people to sign a petition the length of a rainbow, the commander in chief has to resign."

"Really?" Serena looked interested, but then her face dropped. "All Enrico would have to do is get his thugs to tear up the petition."

"Horatio also told us that Enrico used to have all these phobias when he was a boy," said Nicola. "I was thinking maybe we could use those phobias in some way."

"He was frightened of the color yellow, music, buttons, and peanut butter sticking to the roof of his mouth," said Tyler, counting them off on his fingers.

"That was when he was a little boy. He might have grown out of those phobias by now," said Greta.

"I don't think so," said Serena slowly. "When Enrico first came into power he made the Quiet Please Decree. It bans music of all forms—singing, musical instruments, even humming!"

"And he brought in the Anti-Yellow Legislation," said

Joshua. "The penalty for wearing yellow on Shobble is life imprisonment."

"And then there's the Button-Free Regulation!" said Serena. "All clothes have to be made without buttons—only zippers allowed!"

"And we're a peanut-butter-free planet," said Joshua. "I thought Enrico had a peanut allergy but he's just scared of it sticking to the roof of his mouth!"

"So the question is," said Nicola, "could we use all those phobias in some way to help overthrow Enrico?"

"We could organize a big protest march," began Tyler slowly.

"And everyone could wear yellow clothes," said Sean. "And we could all be singing or playing musical instruments!" said Joshua.

"And eating peanut-butter sandwiches!" said Serena.

"I'm allergic," said Greta.

"Okay, well, not everyone," said Serena.

"Don't forget the buttons," said Nicola.

"We could all be wearing *yellow* buttons!" said Shimlara.

"We could present the petition as long as a rainbow at the same time," said a voice from the other side of the cave.

They all looked around. It was Topaz, sitting up in bed and rubbing her eyes.

She threw back the covers and leaped out of bed.

"This could work," she said. "If we got every single person on the planet of Shobble to march, this could totally work."

Joshua tipped his chair back on an angle, linked his hands behind his head, and looked smug. He said, "Told you she wasn't serious about giving up the cause."

31

TOPAZ STOOD AT THE WHITEBOARD WRITING DOWN people's ideas as they called them out. She had to keep stopping to blow her nose and she was sucking on a (chocolate-flavored) cough drop but her depression seemed to have lifted. The vibrant girl in the photo was back. Nicola admired the unselfconscious way Topaz led the group. She wasn't too bossy but at the same time she didn't try too hard to make people like her. When Sean and Joshua started yawning and throwing things at each other in the middle of some long, involved story Greta told about a gymnastics competition that was meant to demonstrate some point, Topaz calmly told Sean and Joshua to stop it and Greta to hurry up. Everyone seemed to respect her. Was it simply because she didn't exhibit any self-doubt? Was being a leader like handling a ferocious dog? "Never let the dog see your fear," Nicola's dad always told her.

"Oh, I'm sorry, Nicola." Topaz caught her eye. "You should be up here, too. You're the leader of the Space Brigade. I'm such a bossy boots."

"Oh, no, that's okay." Nicola felt shy.

"No, no. You and I will be joint leaders of this operation," insisted Topaz. "If it wasn't for you, I'd still be lying in bed feeling sorry for myself."

Nicola went up to the front and took the whiteboard marker that Topaz handed her.

"Okay, what do you think we've forgotten?" asked Topaz.

For a moment, Nicola's mind went blank. *Focus*, she told herself. Katie's encouraging face appeared in her mind, saying, "You can do it, Nic." Nicola realized how stupid it was to be worrying what people thought of her, when Katie was being held hostage, for heaven's sakes! That was all that mattered. Rescuing Katie. Nicola's mind became sharp and clear.

"Okay," she said. "We need to figure out a way to let as many people as possible know about the march. How do we do that?"

"Newspaper," contributed Serena. "It would be great if we could get an article in the newspaper, telling everybody where and when to meet."

"Excellent!" said Nicola and wrote the word *newspaper* up on the whiteboard. She managed to ignore Sean, who was making a cross-eyed face at her, and said, "So how do we get an article in the newspaper?"

"Oh! Oh! Me, me! Pick me!" Shimlara waved both arms around in the air as if Nicola were a teacher.

"Shimlara?" said Nicola, trying to keep a straight face.

"Your pocket! Your pocket! Look in your pocket!"

"My pocket?"

"Your pocket! Your back pocket!"

Nicola didn't know what she was talking about. She gave Topaz an apologetic look as if to say, "Sorry about the Space Brigade's wacky behavior," and slid her hand into her pocket. She pulled out a small white card.

Nicola looked at it without recognition. It said:

JENNY JENKINS

Reporter

THE SHOBBLE TIMES
TIX NO.: 993-9808089108340984098309834089309148130043

Suddenly Nicola remembered the reporter at the gates of Enrico's house. Jenny Jenkins. Wasn't that the name of the person who had written the article about Katie? She was obviously prepared to stand up to Enrico. She would be perfect.

Nicola gave Shimlara a grateful look and handed the card over to Topaz. "This reporter said to call if we needed anything. I'm pretty sure she's on our side."

"Fantastic," said Topaz.

"What's a TIX number?" asked Nicola.

Topaz looked at her with surprise. "They haven't

invented the TIX on Earth yet? It's like an apparatus where you can talk to each other through wires."

"Wow," said Nicola, impressed, until Tyler said, "Umm, Nic, I think we call that the *telephone* on Earth."

"Anyway, it's not relevant," said Tyler. "Enrico cut all the TIX lines for ordinary people years ago. Only hairities can use them. But don't worry, I'll send a message through the Underground Chute. It's a system my supporters use that the hairities don't know about. We use a network of old marshmallow mine shafts." She held out the palm of her hand. "Serena?"

Serena was already handing over a scroll of paper. She was just like a nurse handing over the right instruments before the surgeon asked for them. *Mmmm*, thought Nicola. *Now that's leadership.* She could just imagine Sean's face if she held out her hand and said, "Sean?"

Topaz scribbled something on the piece of parchment. In the meantime, Joshua was addressing a label, *Attention: Jenny Jenkins, Shobble Times*. When Topaz finished writing she handed the parchment to Serena. Serena rolled up the parchment and put it in the tube, which she handed to Joshua. He stuck the label on the tube and walked over to the wall of the cave, moved aside a small rock, and dropped in the tube. It all happened in a matter of seconds.

"You work pretty well together," commented Tyler.

"It's all about teamwork," said Topaz.

"Well the problem is," said Greta, "Nicola doesn't play any team sports. That's why the Space Brigade doesn't have good teamwork."

"We kind of have a rule that we never say negative things about each other," commented Topaz.

"Oh yes, but I don't think that could work for us," said Greta airily. "Some of us have a lot of things to improve, don't we, Nicola?"

Nicola's hand clenched so tight around her marker it flew from her grasp.

"Right," said Topaz hastily. "Moving right along. Now what about your friend Katie? How are we going to rescue her?"

"Actually, that won't be necessary."

Nicola spun around so fast she sent the whiteboard crashing to the ground. There was someone standing at the entrance to the cave. Someone with a big smile on her face. Someone with short shiny brown hair.

If Nicola could have wished for one person in the whole world to be standing in that particular spot it would have been this particular person.

"Katie?" she whispered to herself.

And then she yelled it. *"Katie?!"*

32

IT'S ME," SAID KATIE. "IT'S REALLY ME."

There was a shocked pause followed by gasps, exclamations, and a clatter of chairs and feet as the Space Brigade stampeded toward the cave entrance and Katie.

"I can't believe it," everyone kept saying as they threw their arms around Katie. "I can't believe you're here! How did you escape? How did you get here?"

Sean hugged Katie, ruffled her hair, and smacked her vigorously on the back as if he were trying to save her from choking. Then he suddenly stood back and looked at her suspiciously. "Hey, it really is you, isn't it? You're not about to peel off your face and reveal one of Enrico's security thugs?"

Katie pinched her cheek. "There's only me in here."

But she did look different. There were shadows under her eyes and scratches on her face. Her clothes were wet and dirty. Her new short hairstyle made her neck seem longer and changed the shape of her face. Even though she was filthy and obviously exhausted, she looked somehow more confident and mature than the old Katie.

"Nic, ask her a question only the real Katie could answer," ordered Sean.

"Oh, um, I can't think of one."

"Okay, how's this?" said Katie. "When we were in kindergarten, Tyler, Nicola, and I made a really embarrassing secret pact we've never told anyone—"

"Shhhh!" shouted Tyler and Nicola at the same time. "It's the real Katie!"

Nicola introduced Katie to Topaz, Serena, and Joshua. "I'm impressed that you managed to escape from Enrico's hostage room," said Topaz.

"Oh, well, I had a *lot* of help," said Katie.

"Have some hizza and tell us about it," offered Joshua.

"Hizza!" said Katie. "I was just thinking I could smell hizza!" *Gosh*, thought Nicola. *She sounds like she's been living on Shobble for years.* It gave her a sad, almost jealous feeling thinking of all the things Katie had experienced without her. Would their friendship be changed now?

"Katie, your hair looks great!" said Shimlara. "We were so upset when we heard Enrico had cut it off, but it really suits you."

"*He* didn't cut if off," said Katie with a mouth full of hizza. "That's how all this started. I was just so sick of the whole 'hairity' business, I asked Joy to cut it off for me. You see, I found out there was a Katie Hobbs Fan Club, and that was just too much. Can you think of anything worse—a fan club just for me!" She took another huge bite of hizza.

"I'm pretty sure the girls at school have a secret Sean Berry Fan Club," said Sean. He ran his fingers through his hair like a rock star. "It doesn't worry me."

"Well, I didn't like it. After it was cut I felt great. Then that article appeared in the newspaper and the fan club started holding candlelit vigils outside Enrico's mansion. They were singing songs all about 'letting Katie go' and how I should be free like a bird or something. Anyway, it was driving Enrico nuts. So after I cut my hair he paraded me in front of them, saying, 'Look! She's not even a hairity!' He thought that would be the end of my fan club. The funny thing was—"

Katie stopped and looked shy.

"What?" prompted Nicola.

"Well," said Katie. "They still liked me. Actually, they seemed to like me even more. Enrico couldn't believe it. The problem was that it sent Enrico into a jealous rage. He kept saying to them, 'But why? Why do you like her? Look at her hair! Do you like her more than *me*? Why don't you start a fan club for me?' And when he said that someone laughed. Well, that was it. Enrico decided to starve me."

"Oh no!" said Nicola. "I knew you looked thinner!"

"No, no," said Katie. "Joy and Silent Fred were sneaking

me in plenty of food. Lots of hizza. Also, I'd made friends with some of the security thugs because of our Scrabble games, so they were bringing me food to eat, too. But then Enrico started visiting me to see how much I was suffering and it infuriated him the way I was still smiling. He kept saying to the thugs, 'I want to see her *miserable*! Why doesn't she look *sadder*? She looks happier than my *own children*!' (Well, it wasn't my fault. Those twins are such whiners.) Anyway, Enrico decided the only solution was to reduce my oxygen intake—"

"What?" said Sean. "He tried to suffocate you?"

"Well, that's when Joy and Silent Fred and the Katie Hobbs Fan Club and the nice security thugs all got together and came up with this plan to smuggle me out. They distracted the nasty security thugs with a fake fire and then I had to climb down this rope ladder from my window in the middle of the night—"

"You must have been terrified," said Nicola.

"I was—but it was better than suffocating. They had the most beautiful ShobGobble waiting for me. I had to learn how to ride pretty fast! You have to be really light with your feather-whip, don't you?"

"So you *rode* all the way here on a ShobGobble?" said Greta. "All on your *own*?"

"Yes," said Katie. She gave them a smile but her eyes

looked tired. "I didn't think I could do it but I guess I did. Of course, when I came through the Valley of High Hopes I thought I could do anything! Oh, and when I was in the Valley I came upon this huge family reunion. They said it was all due to the Space Brigade! This old man called Horatio Banks couldn't stop talking about how wonderful you all were. Oh, and a girl called Barb said she hoped your arm was okay, Nicola. What happened to your arm?"

"A Biter," explained Nicola, and then she said, "Hey, does that mean you crossed the Raging River on your own? You had to fight off the Biters *all by yourself*?"

"Yes," said Katie. "But I crossed it at night. Apparently, the Biters can't see as well at night, so you're less likely to be bitten."

"You crossed that river on your own at night," said Tyler. He shook his head. "You are—you are—"

"A legend," completed Sean.

"My hero," completed Shimlara.

"Stop it," said Katie. "That wasn't the worst part. The worst part was when I was crossing the Sweet Dream Swamplands during the hurricane. Although I shouldn't complain. I looked up at one point and saw a hot-air balloon. Can you believe it? It looked like it was going to smash into the mountain. I felt so sorry for those people!"

"That was us!" yelled the Space Brigade as one.

"You're kidding!" said Katie.

"So I guess now you've got Katie back you don't need to help us with the revolution," said Topaz, once they'd all stopped exchanging stories. "You'll probably be wanting to go straight back to Earth."

Nicola was about to answer but Katie got in first. "No way! We have to help you! Silent Fred and Joy are keeping Enrico away by pretending that I've caught some sort of horrible contagious disease, but they won't be able to keep that up forever. Enrico will find out the truth eventually and I don't want anyone to get in trouble because of me when he does."

"That's not your responsibility. We'd understand if you wanted to go straight back to Earth," said Serena.

"We wouldn't just desert you," said Nicola.

"We can't go back to Earth," said Tyler.

"We must do our duty," agreed Nicola. *Our noble duty*, she thought grandly to herself.

"No, I mean we *can't*," said Tyler. "Enrico has still got our spaceship, remember?"

"Oh, that's right," said Nicola. It somehow didn't feel quite so noble once she realized they were trapped on Shobble.

"He's keeping it under his bed," said Shimlara unexpectedly.

"How do you know that?" asked Tyler.

"I remember reading his mind when he took it," said Shimlara. "He thought, *The little peasants will never think to look under my bed.*"

"That's really creepy the way you do that," said Joshua.

At that moment there was a thud of something falling. "Someone's sent us a message through the underground system," said Serena. She walked over to the side of the cave, moved aside a rock, and picked up a tube with a rolled-up parchment inside it.

"Wow. I wish we had a way of contacting each other like that on Earth," said Sean.

"We do," said Tyler patiently. "It's called the *postal system.*"

Serena looked at the parchment and brought it over to Topaz. "It's from that newspaper reporter," she said.

Topaz took the letter. She read a few lines and looked up and smiled. "She's going to run a story about the protest march for us!" She went back to reading and her smile disappeared. She frowned and chewed on her lip.

"What is it?" asked Nicola anxiously.

Topaz looked up again. "Enrico has found out that Katie escaped. He's not happy."

"What do you mean 'not happy'?"

Topaz said, "He's on his way to find us."

33

EVERYONE WHO HELPED KATIE HAS GONE INTO hiding," said Topaz. "Joy, Silent Fred, the nice security thugs, and all of the Katie Hobbs Fan Club."

Katie looked devastated. "I shouldn't have escaped," she said. "I've put them all in danger!"

"It gets worse," said Topaz. "Everyone in this cave has been put on trial for a whole list of crimes. We've all been found guilty."

"What sort of crimes?" asked Nicola.

"Let's see." Topaz looked again at the reporter's letter. "Disobeying a direct order of the commander in chief, impersonating a hairity, stealing a hot-air balloon."

"That's an outrage! A travesty!" said Nicola. She thought for a few seconds. "Although, I guess we are guilty of all those things."

"But we should have a chance to defend ourselves!" said Greta. "How can they have a trial without us even being there?"

"The judge was a hairity," said Topaz. "We've all been sentenced to a lifetime in jail. The security thugs are under orders to capture us, dead or alive. They're on their way here with Enrico. We've got twenty-four hours at the most. And the worst part is, they'll all be armed with despair gas."

"What's despair gas?" asked Katie.

"It's terrible, terrible stuff," said Topaz, which wasn't exactly helpful.

Serena said, "You know how in the Valley of High Hopes you felt filled with hope? Like you could do anything in the world?"

They all nodded.

"Well, despair gas has the opposite effect. One whiff of despair gas and you feel so miserable you want to lie down and give up. It's like how Topaz felt with her cold but far, far worse."

"Can't you just wear masks?" asked Sean. "So you don't breathe it in?"

"It's strong enough to get through any material," said Joshua.

"Well, we'll just have to be stronger than the despair gas," said Nicola. "We'll have to be prepared not to give up, no matter how bad we feel!"

"Yes," said Topaz doubtfully. "Although—" She stopped herself and smiled with difficulty. "No, you're absolutely right."

"Instead of running and hiding from Enrico and the

security thugs, we should go ahead with our original plan of the protest march," said Nicola. She could feel determination filling her chest. "We should meet them head-on! We've got to make use of Enrico's phobias like we said. Let's get back to planning. So we agreed we should all be carrying buttons and wearing yellow—"

"Well, yes, okay, we did say that, but we weren't being practical!" said Topaz irritably. "There are no buttons or yellow clothes on the whole planet of Shobble."

There was a moment of tense silence.

"We could dye our clothes yellow," offered Shimlara.

"Oh yes, because yellow dye is so readily available here on Shobble," said Topaz.

"No need to be sarcastic," said Nicola, surprised.

"Sorry." Topaz looked guilty. She blew her nose hard and said again, "Sorry. I'm just frightened this isn't going to work."

"Okay, well, I guess we can't all wear yellow," said Nicola. "But we can—"

"Chili," Greta interrupted her.

"I beg your pardon?" said Nicola.

"Remember how you meant to pick up a jar of chili from your dad's spice rack and instead you brought turmeric?"

"Yes," said Nicola, wondering why Greta was choosing now to bring up Nicola's past mistakes.

"Well, just the other day my mother called up the Stain Brains—"

"Stain Brains?" interrupted Nicola. Was Greta going a bit mad?

"It's a radio show where a panel of experts tell you how to get stains out of your clothes. It's my mother's favorite show. I find it quite interesting, too. Anyway, my mother called up to see how she could get a bright yellow turmeric stain out of her favorite apron. Turmeric is a *yellow spice*."

Nicola still didn't get it, until Katie said excitedly, "So we could add your jar of turmeric to a big vat of boiling water and easily dye all our clothes yellow!"

"Of course!" said Nicola, pretending she'd understood all along. "Excellent. Well done, Greta. Okay, why don't you and Katie be in charge of dyeing all the clothes yellow?"

"So we're *both* in charge of clothes?" said Greta. "But who has the final authority?"

"Oh, you do, Greta," said Katie, giving Nicola a look.

"Okay, so let's put buttons in the 'too-hard basket' for now," said Nicola. "What other phobias did Enrico have?"

"Music," said Shimlara.

"Screaming Puppies!" said Sean.

"Did he just swear in Earthling language?" asked Joshua.

"No, it's Sean's favorite band," said Nicola.

"We can play the music really loudly when we're marching," said Sean. "That will freak Enrico out."

"We'll need to rig up some sort of loudspeaker," said Tyler.

"You mean a loudtalker?" asked Joshua.

"Are you two talking about a loudshouter?" asked Shimlara. "That's what we call it on Globagaskar."

"Okay, you boys are in charge of music," said Nicola. As she wrote their names up on the whiteboard, she caught sight of Topaz watching her intently.

"You're a really good leader," said Topaz. "I could learn a lot from you."

"Oh, thanks." Suddenly the pen felt clumsy in Nicola's hand and she didn't know what to say or do next. It was just like when she was learning to ride a bike and her dad called out, "You're doing great!" and Nicola immediately went lopsided and fell off.

Topaz put her hand on Nicola's arm. "Do you really think we can do this? Do you think we can beat Enrico?"

An image of a laughing Enrico surrounded by hundreds of huge security thugs came into Nicola's head.

No, she thought. *No way can we beat him!*

But out loud she said, "Yes. Of course, we can beat him—and we will."

34

The Shobble Times

SPECIAL LATE EDITION

ENRICO—THE PEOPLE OF SHOBBLE SAY IT'S TIME TO GO!

BY JENNY JENKINS

The time has come for the people of Shobble to let Enrico know that we've had **ENOUGH**. We've had **ENOUGH** of mining and drilling night and day for the ShobbleChoc that fills your treasure accounts, while we earn nothing—not even your praise! We've had **ENOUGH** of watching your spoiled children prance about in satin and lace, while our children don't even have **SOCKS**! We've had **ENOUGH** of seeing lovely things such as the Department of Free Goods and Services taken away. We've had **ENOUGH** of your strange laws such as the Quiet Please Decree. We've had **ENOUGH** of this planet's ridiculous obsession with hairities (although see page **27** for this reporter's scoop on beautiful Melanie Melanoid and the Love

Rat who broke her heart!). We've had enough of your security thugs, your cruelty, your vanity, and your fake charm!

If all this rings true with you, then here is your chance to take ACTION! The infamous Topaz Silverbell and her associates, together with Nicola Berry and the Space Brigade (Earthling visitors who have been shocked by the state of our planet! Embarrassed? You should be!) have organized a protest march to take place at 10 a.m. tomorrow morning starting at the Honey Sea Wharf. They are calling upon every man, woman, and child to stand up and be counted. You will be asked to sign a petition calling for Enrico's resignation. You don't need to bring anything except your PASSION FOR CHANGE and a packed lunch.

Be there or be square! (A traditional Earthling catchphrase.)

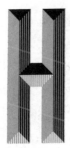

OW MANY PEOPLE DO YOU THINK WILL COME?" asked Nicola. The special edition of the newspaper had just arrived through the chute and been passed around to everyone to read.

"I don't know," said Topaz. "Maybe a few hundred? Maybe just us? I don't know."

"Well, how many Topaz supporters are there on the planet of Shobble?" asked Greta. "I assume you keep a database."

"We have no idea how many supporters we have," said

Serena. "You don't realize the level of fear people have suffered under Enrico's regime. There may be people out there who support Topaz but have never been brave enough to say it aloud."

"I wonder if Enrico has read this yet," said Shimlara.

"He will have." Topaz grimaced. "He'll be waiting for us at the Honey Sea Wharf with his security thugs. You can be sure of that."

There was silence for a few seconds as everyone tried to imagine what it would be like the following morning.

"By this time tomorrow night, we could be celebrating Enrico's resignation!" said Katie optimistically.

"Or we could be in jail," said Sean.

The mood in the cave became gloomy.

"Maybe this isn't such a good idea," said Serena hesitantly. "If nobody turns up for the protest march, then we're basically just giving ourselves up to Enrico and his thugs. We might be better off going into hiding."

"No," said Topaz. "This is it. This is our last chance to stand up to Enrico. I understand if you choose not to be there."

"I'm not a *coward*, Topaz!" said Serena irritably. "I'm just—"

"Delivery for you!"

Everyone jumped at the sound of a cheerful voice at the entry to the cave.

"I thought nobody knew this cave was here!" whispered Nicola.

"Only our families," whispered back Topaz.

"Just need a signature!" called out the voice again.

"It could be a trick," whispered Joshua. "It might be one of Enrico's thugs."

"Urgent delivery for Nicola Berry from Mr. H. Banks!" called out the voice, a little less cheerfully. "It's quite cold out here!"

Nicola jumped to her feet. "It's something from Horatio!" she explained. "The old man from the Valley of High Hopes."

Topaz helped her push aside the rock at the entrance to the cave. A Shobble man dressed in a courier's uniform and carrying a clipboard said, "Take your own sweet time, ladies! Sign here."

Nicola signed on the dotted line and the man gestured behind him at a huge pile of boxes.

"Where do you want 'em?"

"What are they?" asked Nicola.

"Don't ask me," said the courier. "Oh, by the way, the animals are over there."

"Animals?"

"Five frisky ShobGobbles," said the courier. "Seemed in a hurry to get here."

Nicola's heart did a cartwheel. "Quicksilver!" she cried and ran over to bury her face in his feathery mane. Quicksilver chirped and butted Nicola gently with his head, his three eyes filled with such warmth and wisdom that Nicola's own eyes filled with happy tears. "I missed you! I'm so glad to see you!"

As she caressed him, she found a small white envelope under his saddle. She opened it and read.

Dearest Nicola,

THANK YOU from the bottom of my heart for reuniting me with my family. Although the back of my head is still aching somewhat from where my beloved wife gave me a well deserved slap when she first saw me, I am blissfully happy. It turns out that my family can't even remember the details of our argument. They are just angry with me for disappearing. (Of course, I actually CAN remember the details and I remain convinced that I was in the right, but I think it may be prudent to keep that to myself.)

My granddaughter Barb tells me that you suffered a Biter wound while crossing the Raging River. I do hope it is not giving you too much pain.

The entire Banks family would like to be of service to you in any way at all. For example, it may interest you to know that we once owned a thriving business called BANKS' BEAUTIFUL BUTTONS. We still have a lot of old stock available and it occurred to me that it could come in handy to you.

Also, Barb happened to be in the Why Not Drop Inn stables today, where she found your ShobGobbles sleeping. She was able to give them some Wake-UpBiotics and we thought you might like them returned to you.

Yours sincerely,
Horatio Banks

P.S. You may be wondering how we obtained this address. Barb's mother went to school with a lady who plays Shobble-Ball with a lady who is in a Recipe Swap Club with a lady who lives next door to Topaz's mother—and she was able to pass on Topaz's details. So her security is not in any way compromised. Topaz's mother asked if you could please ask Topaz and Joshua to bundle up tomorrow and keep their ears covered, as the wind can be so cold this time of year.

"Shobgobby!" It was Shimlara running out from the cave.

She was followed by Tyler calling out fondly, "Fleet-foot!" and Sean hollering, "Lethal Weapon!" Even Greta hurried out and said, "Hey, *you*!" to her ShobGobble.

Topaz, Serena, and Joshua were busy opening the boxes that Horatio had sent.

"Buttons!" called out Joshua. He lifted up a handful of chunky, brightly colored buttons and let them fall through his fingers.

"Thousands and thousands of extremely *scary* buttons!" cried Topaz and Serena, plunging their hands deep into the boxes.

"Well, you folks seem pretty happy with your delivery," said the courier. "I'll be on my way."

As he went to climb on to his ShobGobble he said casually, "Let's hope tomorrow is a nice day." He winked and pushed back his hair so they could clearly see the tiny *t* on his forehead. "A *very* nice day."

35

THERE IS NOBODY HERE," SAID TOPAZ FRANTIcally. "Do you think—"

Nicola interrupted her. "It's only nine-thirty a.m. They'll be here." She tried to sound as if she really believed it.

It was the following morning and the Space Brigade, Topaz, Serena, and Joshua were all sitting astride their ShobGobbles at the deserted Honey Sea Wharf. They had left Topaz's cave at dawn and made their way down the Cloud-Capped Mountain. It had been a beautiful morning. As their ShobGobbles crunched their way through the snow (quite slowly, because they were laden down with supplies for the day ahead), their moods had been upbeat. Sean and Joshua had made up a stupid song that they all chanted over and over again:

"Enrico, Enrico, your day has come!
Enrico, Enrico, get ready to run!
We know all your phobias, every single one!
Enrico, Enrico, your day has come!"

"The rhyme could be improved," Greta had commented, but even she had joined in. Now the day was still beautiful, but their moods had become serious as they all looked silently out at the Honey Sea, which was frozen, like all of Shobble's seas at this time of year according to Serena. There was a huge frozen wave just near the wharf. It must have been just about to crash down when the temperatures plummeted and the sea froze. Now it was an incredible, translucent green ice sculpture.

Sean squinted his eyes at something in the distance. "What's that over there?"

There was a cloud of bobbing black dots on the horizon.

"They're Enrico's flags," said Topaz. Her face was pale. "They're coming."

Joshua looked at his watch. "I estimate it will take them about two hours to get here."

"We'd better set everything up for the protest march," said Nicola.

"Nobody is coming," said Greta emphatically.

"Of course they're coming!" said Katie, but Nicola could tell by the way she was clenching her hands that she was trying hard not to chew at her nails.

"If nobody comes," said Greta, "we've got no chance—"

"Here comes somebody!" cried Tyler.

They all turned and saw a lone figure walking toward them. The person was struggling under the weight of a gigantic scroll of rose-colored parchment.

"It must be that reporter," said Topaz. "She promised she'd bring the parchment for the petition."

They all climbed down from their ShobGobbles and hurried over to help her.

Jenny Jenkins beamed at them. She had pinned her hair back from her forehead so her *t* tattoo was clearly visible, and she looked ready for action.

"We've got a perfect day for it," she said. She looked around her. "Um, where is everybody?"

"We don't know," said Nicola. "We're just starting to feel a bit nervous."

"Oh, no need to be nervous," said Jenny nervously. "People will come. You saw my article, right? I mean, everybody on the planet reads the *Shobble Times*. We must surely get *some* people to turn up."

"Well, we've brought along this table for people to line up and sign the petition," said Topaz. "So I guess we should set it all up."

"And we'll organize the music," said Sean.

"I guess we can get the yellow dye ready for people's clothes," said Greta. "Even though I'm sure nobody is coming."

Jenny took a pen out from behind her ear and began to take notes. "So you're dyeing everyone's clothes yellow because you believe Enrico is frightened of the color yellow?"

"Yes, he has xanthophobia," said Nicola.

"Gosh. How do you spell that?" asked Jenny, and without waiting for an answer she said, "And aren't everyone's clothes going to be wet after you dye them?"

"I've got an instant clothes dryer," said Shimlara.

"I've never heard of such a thing."

"It's from the planet of Globagaskar," said Shimlara. "That's where I'm from."

"Oh, this is such a *scoop*." Jenny sighed happily.

"So let's dye your clothes first, Jenny," said Greta. She and Katie were busy pouring Nicola's jar of turmeric into a big pot of boiling water. "We've set up this changing room here for you." She pointed at a small tent.

"Oh." Jenny looked down sadly at her navy blue jacket. "Yellow really isn't my color. Although I guess I shouldn't be worried about having a pasty complexion when we're in the middle of the revolution."

"No, that would be selfish," agreed Greta.

"Nicola!"

Nicola saw a sleigh pull up beside her. It was Horatio. He had the sleigh reins in one hand and the other arm around a tiny, rather stern-faced old woman. Horatio had changed a lot since they'd seen him in the forest. He could no longer be mistaken for a shrub. His face was rounder, his hair washed, and he was wearing clean clothes.

"This is the young Earthling who brought us back together," said Horatio. "Nicola, I'd like you to meet my wife, Bertha Banks."

Bertha's wrinkled face was transformed as she smiled at Nicola. "Thank you so much for tracking down my foolish husband." She cuffed Horatio on the back of his head and Horatio gave her a kiss on the cheek.

"Did you get my delivery, Nicola?" asked Horatio.

"Oh yes, thank you!" said Nicola. "Wait till you see what we've got planned for the buttons!"

"I can't wait," said Horatio. He looked around at all the activity approvingly. "And I see we're all going to be wearing yellow. Naughty Enrico is going to be in a terrible state! He'll be sobbing and calling for his mother!"

"Well, let's hope so," said Nicola doubtfully. Horatio couldn't seem to get it into his head that Enrico had grown up.

"Excuse me, Mr. Banks, sir!" called out Serena. She was sitting at the table with the rose-colored scroll of parchment. "Would you like to be first to sign the petition?"

"It would be my honor," said Horatio. He silently read the petition. Nicola knew what it said, because she and Serena had been up late the night before trying to work out the exact wording. They had finally decided upon:

We the undersigned, representing the people of Shobble,

respectfully call for the immediate resignation of the commander in chief, Enrico, as is our right under clause number 367-AAB-38479579034554 of Shobble's constitution. We do this because of his cruelty to our people, his selfishness, his vanity, and his general lack of good leadership qualities.

"Perfect," said Horatio. He wrote his name with a flourish at the top of the petition and his wife did the same.

"We're going to need a few more people to show up today if we're going to get a petition as long as a rainbow," commented Serena.

"Oh, they'll come," said Horatio. "The people of Shobble know when enough is enough. They'll come. In fact, look—here comes my granddaughter."

Barb arrived with the siren around her forehead blaring. "Sorry I'm late!" she shouted over the siren. She turned it off. "Let me have a quick look at that Biter wound, Nicola. Oh, good, it's healing nicely. Ummm—is this all of us? Not that I'm complaining or anything."

"We're hoping for a few more people," admitted Nicola.

There was another jangle of sleigh bells and Nicola looked up to see two familiar, smiling faces. It was Joy and Silent Fred.

They ran over and hugged everybody.

"Oh, I'm so proud of both you girls," said Joy, with one

arm around Katie and another around Nicola. Silent Fred wrote on his blackboard, THIS IS THE BEST DAY OF MY LIFE, and kept jabbing at it with his finger to reinforce the point.

Next came a sleigh with a banner reading THE KATIE HOBBS FAN CLUB. A group of people got out and went running over to Katie. Nicola recognized at least two of the security thugs from Enrico's house, except that they were now wearing jolly sweaters with pictures of reindeers instead of black T-shirts, and one of them was calling out, "Guess what, Katie! I'm starting Shobble's first Scrabble tournament!"

Right behind the Katie Hobbs Fan Club was another sleigh with a plump pink-faced woman and a tall gentle-looking man. Nicola realized they were Topaz and Joshua's parents when she heard the woman say, "Topaz and Joshua Silverbell—what are you children *wearing*? You will *freeze* to *death*."

As everyone arrived Katie and Greta efficiently organized for their clothes to be dyed yellow. Shimlara ran them through her instant clothes dryer and the people dressed in the changing tent, emerging minutes later in their bright yellow clothes. Meanwhile, Sean and Joshua were rigging up loudspeakers (or loudtalkers or loudshouters, depending on which planet you're from) for the music and Tyler was busy making the final arrangements for the plan they'd come up with for the buttons.

Nicola went over to Serena's table to see how the petition was coming along.

"It's about the length of my arm," said Serena, holding it up. "Not *quite* the length of a rainbow."

Topaz came and stood beside them. "This is great," she began. "But—"

"But we need more people," finished Nicola. She looked around her. They now had enough people for quite a good party but it wasn't enough for a protest march and it certainly wasn't enough to intimidate Enrico.

"The security thugs will just round us all up and take us to jail," fretted Topaz. "If more people don't show up soon I'm wondering if we should cancel the whole thing and just *run*—run for our lives!"

"Oh my goodness," said Serena.

"Well, I'm serious," said Topaz.

"No—oh my goodness, *look*!" Serena pointed over their shoulders. Topaz and Nicola turned around. Topaz made a sound that was somewhere between a sob, a laugh, and a hiccup. Nicola pressed both her hands to her cheeks.

There was a great swarming mass coming across the foothills of the Cloud-Capped Mountain.

It was the people of Shobble.

There were families crammed into slow-moving sleighs. There were young people riding ShobGobbles and old people being pushed in wheelchairs. There were mothers with babies in strollers and fathers with children on their shoulders. There were marshmallow miners and chocolate drillers with their tools still in their hands and determined expressions on their grimy faces. There were even *hairities*—their long brown hair flying glamorously behind them as they marched toward the Honey Sea Wharf.

As Nicola looked toward the horizon she could see even more people.

"It must be the whole planet," whispered Topaz. Her eyes were like saucers.

It seemed that the people of Shobble were ready to have their say.

I T WAS MAYHEM. THERE WERE FAR TOO MANY PEOPLE.
Far too many helpful, chatty, overexcited people. Too
many people with questions. Too many people with
opinions.

A jostling crowd surrounded Nicola and Topaz.

"Are you *sure* Enrico has a phobia about the color
yellow? Because I heard it was the color red."

"My son signed the petition but he forgot to put his
middle name. Should he sign it again?"

"Is Katie Hobbs really here?"

"Are you really Topaz Silverbell? Can I touch you?"

"Are you really an Earthling? Can I touch you?"

"Is it true that tall girl comes from Globagaskar?"

"Where are the toilets?"

"Have you seen my daughter?"

"Have you seen my son?"

"Where should I go after I've signed the petition?"

"Is morning tea provided?"

"Is it true Enrico is on his way?"

Topaz and Nicola did their best to answer everyone's
questions, but it was impossible.

"This is out of control," said Topaz helplessly.

Nicola looked around her. It felt like they were in the middle of some sort of crazy funfair. Children had converted their shoes into ice skates and were playing on the frozen sea shouting, "Whoopeee!" as they skated dangerously off the crests of the waves. Some teenagers had started a game of Head Crunch in the snow. Adults were standing around in groups, deep in conversation. Mothers swapped recipes. Fathers compared sleigh models. Babies cried. ShobGobbles chirped.

Greta was screeching at people like a demented teacher. "No! I said line up *here*, not *there*! No, we do *not* offer any other color options, I don't care if pink is your favorite color!" It was pandemonium.

Joshua pushed his way through the crowd to where Nicola and Topaz were standing. He pointed across the Honey Sea to the bobbing black flags that marked Enrico's progress. "They're making good time. We've got to get *organized*!"

Horatio was nearby, sitting on a foldout chair next to his wife. He pulled on Nicola's sleeve and she bent down to listen to him. "You two girls have got to take control," he said. "Now."

Nicola stood up and looked around her helplessly. *But how?* She thought of her school principal, Mr. Nix, nervously adjusting his tie on school assembly days, when teachers, parents, and students would all be milling about, cheerfully ignoring him as he pleaded into the microphone, "Could I have a bit of quiet?" For the first time in her life Nicola actually felt sorry for him.

She said to Joshua, "Topaz and I will need microphones."

Joshua looked at her blankly.

"So people can hear us."

"Oh, you mean *macro*phones," said Joshua. "Right. No problem."

"We really need some sort of a stage," said Topaz.

Sean, who was standing near Joshua, said, "Maybe you could fly up on your ShobGobbles over people's heads."

Minutes later, Topaz and Nicola were hovering over the crowd on their ShobGobbles.

Topaz spoke into her macrophone. "Can I have your attention, please?"

No one took the slightest notice.

"Ladies and gentlemen," tried Nicola. The crowd ignored her.

Nicola and Topaz looked at each other and nodded.

"Stop talking and listen up!" they thundered simultaneously.

There was silence. Even the babies stopped crying.

Topaz said, "My name is Topaz Silverbell and this is Nicola Berry from the planet Earth and we want to thank you for coming today."

There was thunderous applause and calls of "Topaz! Topaz!" and "Hey there, Earthling!" A miner with a bandage across his nose called out, "I forgive you for the fizz-bang bomb, Topaz!"

"Thank you," said Topaz. "But this is serious. We need to be ready for Enrico and the security thugs. We believe they will be armed with despair gas."

This was met with a ripple of dismay. Nicola could hear people saying things like, "We can't win against despair gas," and "Maybe we should go home."

Topaz looked a little despairing herself so Nicola took over.

"Despair is just a feeling," she said.

"A pretty serious feeling," called out a rough-looking chocolate driller.

"Yes, but just because you feel something doesn't mean you have to give in to that feeling. We've got to stay strong! Besides which, we've got *people power*!" Nicola punched a fist in the air. There was silence, apart from someone saying clearly, "What's she doing with her fist in the air like that?"

Nicola dropped her arm and said, "We've got *weapons* to fight Enrico!"

That cheered everyone up considerably. *"Yeah!"* shouted a group of teenage boys.

Nicola decided not to mention that their only weapons were yellow clothes, music, buttons, and a jar of peanut butter.

"So if this is going to work we need you to follow our orders exactly," said Topaz. "We need you to first join the clothes-dyeing line and then move on to the petition-signing line. After that, we need you to line up in rows with your arms linked."

"And be quiet," added Nicola.

"Are there any questions?" asked Topaz.

A portly miner put his hand up. "When is lunch?"

"Straight after we've overthrown Enrico," said Nicola quickly. "Any more questions?"

There was silence. Nicola saw Topaz's father discreetly trying to take their photo, while Topaz's mother called out, "Oh, well done, darlings!" It was lucky her own parents were safely on Earth where they couldn't embarrass her.

"Right," said Topaz. "Let's do it!"

It was a miracle. People actually did as they were told. Without fuss, they lined up in front of Katie and Greta to have their clothes dyed and then stood in line to sign the petition. A short time later, rows of Shobble people, dressed from head to toe in yellow (quite a few had obligingly offered to dye their hair yellow as well, to help make themselves scarier to Enrico) began to form, their arms linked, quietly chatting to one another. Meanwhile, Serena rolled out more and more of the scroll of parchment for the petition.

An hour later, only a few stragglers remained to sign.

"Do you think it's as long as a rainbow yet?" asked Nicola.

"I think it might just make it," said Serena.

And that's when Joshua spoke the chilling words, "They're here."

37

**ICOLA'S HEART WAS PUMPING LIKE SOME**
sort of out-of-control machine. She could feel
Quicksilver's muscles tense beneath her, and
she caressed his mane, trying to calm both the
animal and herself.

This was it. If they failed today, they would all be stuck
in a Shobble jail forever. She would never see Earth or her
bedroom or her parents again.

She and the Space Brigade, together with Topaz,
Serena, and Joshua, were all astride their ShobGobbles,
their feather-whips held in front of them. Behind them
the yellow-dressed people of Shobble stood, arms linked,
looking like a massive field of yellow corn.

There was a sound of thundering hooves. Enrico and
his security thugs were approaching swiftly around the
curved snowy shore of the Honey Sea. They were riding
black ShobGobbles and brandishing black feather-whips.
Enrico rode at the front, wearing a bloodred cape tied
around his neck that billowed behind him. He was followed
by a pack of enormous, barrel-chested security thugs, with
silver canisters strapped to their backs.

"Those canisters are filled with despair gas," said Topaz.

"He's brought more thugs than I expected," said Joshua.

"We can take them on," said Sean, and only Nicola, who knew her brother so well, could sense the fear and doubt in his voice.

"I can't believe it. He's brought his family along to watch the show!" said Shimlara.

Traveling alongside the thugs was a majestic-looking sleigh. As it got closer, Nicola could see Carmelita and the twins, sitting comfortably back beneath furs and munching on sandwiches as if they were about to watch a soccer match.

"What should we do?" asked Katie as Enrico got close enough so that they could see his thin white face.

"Don't move," said Topaz quietly. "Just wait for Nicola or me to give the order."

"Halt!" Enrico commanded his thugs. They instantly pulled up their ShobGobbles and stopped in a precise line behind Enrico, their faces blank and robotic.

"Hello, *ladies*," said Enrico, looking at Nicola and Topaz. "I see the incompetent Earthling and the impudent troublemaker have made friends. How sweet! Well, you'll have plenty of time to chat when you spend the rest of your days in a jail cell. Oh, wait a minute, how silly of me! You won't be able to *chat* because you won't be able to *talk* after you've had a lovely, refreshing drink of my specially brewed lemonade!"

There were peals of appreciative laughter from the sleigh.

"We just won't drink it," muttered Sean.

Enrico said, "Oh, it's surprising what you'll drink when you're dying of thirst. Just ask Silent Fred."

Nicola could feel the anger rising from Topaz and Joshua like steam from a kettle.

"What do you think of our clothes, Enrico? Do you like the *color*? We've gone for a lovely buttery, lemony, sun-shiny *yellow*," said Nicola.

At the same moment everyone dropped their feather-whips so Enrico could see their dyed clothes.

Enrico's head snapped back as if he'd been slapped.

"Yellow!" He looked nauseated. He pointed a trembling finger at them and averted his head. "You are all in viola-tion of the Anti-Yellow Legislation!"

"Look behind us, Enrico," said Topaz. "So is the whole planet."

"What are you talking about?" Enrico snapped.

Nicola, Topaz, and the others led their ShobGobbles aside, like a curtain opening on a stage.

"Wha—" Enrico nearly fell from his ShobGobble. He

dropped his feather-whip and held up his hands as though he were shielding his eyes from the sun. He gibbered to himself. "Yellow. Yucky yellow. Yucky, yucky yellow."

"Ah, I beg your pardon, sir, but are you okay?" asked the largest of the security thugs.

"Darling?" called out Carmelita from the sleigh. "What is it? What's wrong?"

Enrico looked like he was suffering from a bad case of car sickness. He lifted his chin as though to check that he hadn't imagined such a horrible sight and then scrunched his eyes shut in horror. "All my people! My people all dressed in yucky, yucky yellow!"

"It's time to resign, Enrico," said Topaz. "Your people have had enough."

"Never!" said Enrico, but he looked as though he were concentrating hard on not vomiting.

"Um, sir, what would you like us to do?" asked the biggest security thug.

"Des—" began Enrico, but he couldn't get the word out. He wiped a hand across his sweaty forehead.

"Dessert?" tried the security thug. "You feel like dessert? I don't know if now is the time, sir."

Enrico shook his head in frustration. "Desp—"

"Despicable!" said the security thug. "Yes, sir, I agree. What they've done is quite despicable. That's a good point."

"Desp—" tried Enrico again, before retching.

It was so obvious that Enrico was trying to say the words *despair gas* that Nicola nearly said it for him. Instead, she said, "Start the music, boys."

Sean and Joshua nodded.

Seconds later the rhythmic sound of the Screaming Puppies singing their number one hit, "Snakebite," filled the air.

The people of Shobble, who hadn't heard music for over twenty years, lifted their heads in confused delight and began to move to the beat, their arms still linked.

Enrico clapped his hands over his ears and fell forward over his ShobGobble's neck.

"Well, really, darling, whatever is the matter?" called out his wife from the sleigh.

"Music!" Enrico spoke through clenched teeth. "Mucky music! It hurts my ears! Stop that music! You are disobeying the Quiet Please Decree!"

"Although it's actually quite catchy, sir," said the lead security thug, nodding his head in time to the music.

"Mucky music and yucky yellow! Make it stop!"

Sean grinned at Nicola. "Told you that Screaming Puppies album would come in handy."

"Despair gas!" choked out Enrico. "Spray . . . them . . . with . . . despair . . . gas!"

"Yes, sir!" The security thugs reached behind their backs for their canisters.

"Brace yourselves," said Topaz.

How bad could it be? thought Nicola as the thugs lifted long nozzles and sprayed the air with enormous thick black clouds.

A nasty smell filled Nicola's nostrils. It was a sludgy, slimy smell that seemed to travel up her nostrils and straight into her brain.

I'm fine, thought Nicola. *I'm—*

Suddenly a feeling of terrible sadness ballooned through her chest. *What were we thinking? We'll never beat Enrico.*

She looked behind her and saw that the Shobble people were bent backward, like flowers in a breeze. Topaz sat limply in her saddle like a broken puppet. Sean had his face buried in his hands. Even Quicksilver slumped beneath Nicola.

Shimlara slowly rode her ShobGobble up next to Nicola. Her eyes were shiny with tears.

"We can't beat Enrico," she said dully. "We might as well accept it."

"Yes," said Nicola. "Yes, of course, you're right."

"Remember what you said! Despair is just a feeling, Nicola!" called out a voice from the crowd. Nicola recognized the quivery voice of Horatio Banks.

But I was wrong, Horatio. It's not just a feeling. It's crushed glass behind my eyes. It's a weight pressing on my chest.

"Don't give up! *Please*, don't give up!" This time it sounded like Joy. Nicola pressed her face against Quicksilver's feathery neck and remembered Joy's sad face as she sat in the bathroom at Enrico's mansion, telling them about Silent Fred.

There was another voice trying to get her attention. A tiny, mouselike voice.

Try.

It was Nicola's own voice speaking from a corner of her mind, as if from very far away.

I've got to at least try.

But it's too hard. The feeling is too big. It's like a giant, black, hairy animal, sitting on top of me, suffocating me.

So fight it.

FIGHT IT!

And just like that, Nicola proudly lifted her head and resumed her mission.

38

KNOW YOU FEEL REALLY BAD RIGHT NOW BUT I NEED you to fly. Can you do that for me? Please?" Nicola whispered in Quicksilver's ear.

Quicksilver lifted his head slightly. He sighed as if he was exhausted, but then he flapped his wings and carried Nicola into the air. The two hovered above the crowd, Quicksilver breathing heavily. Nicola still had the macrophone from earlier. She pulled it out and began to chant. Her voice trembled and cracked.

"Enrico, Enrico, your day has come!
Enrico, Enrico, get ready to run!
We know all your phobias, every single one!
Enrico, Enrico, your day has come!"

Nothing happened. Quicksilver weakly flapped his wings and Nicola watched the people below, sobbing, wailing, or simply lying on the ground, as if flattened by despair.

Nicola took a deep breath and tried again. "Enrico, Enrico . . ."

She saw Topaz lift her head with difficulty. A minute later Topaz was up in the air on her ShobGobble next to Nicola.

"What are we doing?" asked Topaz. Her face seemed lined with exhaustion, like that of a much older woman.

"I'm not sure," admitted Nicola. "I remember reading somewhere about the power that's created when a whole crowd of people chant together. It's worth a try."

Topaz smiled weakly.

"Enrico, Enrico . . ."

As their two voices melded together, they became louder and stronger.

They were joined next by Katie, followed by Sean, Shimlara, and the others.

Then slowly, one by one, the people of Shobble lifted their heads, straightened up, and joined in the chant. The sound of their voices began to boom across the countryside.

Frowns cleared. People began to smile and then laugh.

"It's gone!" shouted someone. "The despair is gone!"

Enrico's face was a mask of fear and disgust. "Why isn't the despair gas working?" he cried at the thugs. "What have you fools done wrong?"

Nicola looked at Topaz. "Time for the buttons?"

"You bet," said Topaz. "Everybody into formation!"

They all flew their ShobGobbles into a tight circle directly over the top of Enrico's head.

"Fire!" ordered Nicola.

They pulled out the straps on the clever contraptions that Tyler had rigged up on either side of their saddles. Thousands of Horatio's buttons were released into the air.

"A little gift courtesy of Banks' Beautiful Buttons!" yelled out Joshua.

Enrico looked up and his face crumpled.

"It's *raining* buttons!" he cried as the buttons tumbled down all around him, catching in his hair and clothes. Enrico batted them away as if they were maggots. "Beastly buttons! Beastly buttons!"

As the buttons continued to fall, Enrico writhed about so much he toppled off his ShobGobble into the snow, where he rolled about sobbing and hiccuping like a toddler who doesn't want to go to bed.

His security thugs looked appalled by their commander in chief's behavior. "Um, sir?" said the leader. "They're just *buttons*."

"*Yucky* yellow! *Mucky* music! *Beastly* buttons!"

Enrico's family didn't seem capable of speaking. They just sat in their sleigh and stared.

"Hey, Enrico?" shouted Sean. He pulled out the jar of peanut butter from his coat pocket and flew his Shob-Gobble down so he was hovering just over Enrico's head.

"Feeling hungry? Want a nice peanut butter sandwich?" Sean stuck his finger in the jar. "Mmmm, mmm. It's especially sticky peanut butter. It could *easily* get stuck on the roof of your mouth!"

"AAAAAAGGGGGGGHHHHHHHHHHHHH!"

Enrico rolled over so he was facedown in the snow.

"Do you resign, Enrico?" Nicola called out.

Enrico lifted his head. *"Never!"*

"Turn up the music, Sean," said Topaz.

The sound of the Screaming Puppies boomed so loud cracks started to appear in the frozen sea. Enrico desperately tried to plug his ears with handfuls of snow.

"Do you resign?" cried Serena.

"But I don't *want* to!" moaned Enrico.

"Okay, then," said Nicola. "I guess it's time we bombarded you with these *extra large, bright yellow buttons*!"

Enrico's face contorted with horror.

"We don't have any extra large, bright yellow buttons!" hissed Joshua out of the side of his mouth.

"He doesn't know that," hissed back Nicola.

Joshua grinned. She raised her voice.

"Oh, Enrico, how about if we dip these *big yellow buttons* in some *extra sticky peanut butter*!"

Enrico flipped back over on his stomach and buried his face in the snow.

"Gish mish shign! Shign!"

"We didn't quite catch that?" Nicola called out.

Enrico lifted his chin. "Okay, okay, I resign! I resign! Just keep those yucky yellow buttons away from me!"

The crowd roared. Babies were thrown in the air. Couples kissed.

"Success!" cried Serena.

"Whooopeee!" shouted Sean and Joshua, giving each other high fives.

"Oh, thank goodness," said Katie. "I was starting to feel really sorry for him."

Shimlara leaned over from her ShobGobble and hugged Nicola. "Looks like another successful mission for the Space Brigade!"

"Wait just a *minute*!"

It was Topaz. She was speaking into her macrophone and looked fierce and determined.

"Enrico, I don't want to just *bully* you into resigning!"

"Why not?" said Sean.

"Yeah, I don't see the problem," said Joshua.

Enrico sat back up in the snow, shuddering when his hand came in contact with the buttons that were scattered all around him. He looked up at Topaz. His eyes narrowed.

"So you *don't* want me to resign?"

"I want to do it legally," said Topaz. "We have a petition here calling for your resignation. According to the constitution if we present you with a petition as long as a rainbow, then you must resign."

"Fine. Just get it over with," said Enrico sulkily.

"Serena," said Topaz. "Let's see if that petition is the length of a rainbow."

Serena lowered her voice. "But Topaz, what if it's *not*?"

"I don't care. I want this done properly," said Topaz. "You understand, don't you, Nicola?"

"Sort of," said Nicola. She guessed it made sense to force Enrico's resignation legally, rather than just by exploiting his phobias.

"This is ridiculous," huffed Greta.

"That rainbow there might be a good one," said Tyler, pointing at one that began at the Honey Sea Wharf and curved across the crowd of Shobble people. Nicola knew that Tyler would have quickly picked out the shortest rainbow he could see.

Serena took the huge roll of rose-pink paper from her backpack and handed it to Topaz.

"Will you do the honors, Nicola?" asked Topaz.

"Sure," said Nicola nervously. She took a firm hold of the scroll of paper, while Topaz took the other end . . .

"You ready?"

"Yes."

"Let's go."

They flew off in opposite directions to the ends of the rainbow. Nicola looked over her shoulder and saw the rose-pink parchment unfurling out between herself and Topaz like an endless party streamer.

She could see where the rainbow curved to the ground just in front of the Honey Sea Wharf. She urged Quicksilver on with a gentle touch of her feather.

They flew toward the ground and Nicola felt the petition pulling in her hand.

She glanced back and saw that Topaz had already stopped on her ShobGobble at the other end of the rainbow.

Nicola's heart stopped as she looked down at the scroll of pink parchment.

It couldn't be true.

There were no more names on the petition. There was only blank parchment in front of her. They needed about a dozen more signatures. If only everyone had written their names in big capital letters they would have been fine!

She tugged gently on the parchment and felt Topaz tugging it back at the other end. They couldn't stretch it any farther. The petition wasn't long enough. They were very, very close—but not close enough.

"Ha ha ha ha ha!"

The awful sound echoed across the snowy plain.

Enrico had climbed back to his feet, put his hands on his hips, and was laughing hysterically.

39

T WAS ALL OVER.

Nicola could see the pack of security thugs galloping on their black ShobGobbles over to get her, their long greasy hair flying behind them.

There was nowhere to run. Nowhere to hide.

"You've been a good friend," Nicola whispered in Quicksilver's ear.

There were about fifty thugs coming toward Nicola. In fact, it seemed every single one of them was on his way over to her.

Gosh, thought Nicola. If she hadn't been terrified, she would have been flattered. They must really have believed she was an evil Earthling if they thought it would take that many of them to capture her.

"It's okay! I surrender! I surrender!" she called out to the thug leader as he got closer.

He shouted, "Give me that petition!" and held out his hand.

Nicola handed over the scroll.

"Can I trouble you for a pen?"

Nicola thought she must have misheard him. "I beg your pardon?"

"It's just that I don't have one on me," said the leader, patting his shirt pockets.

Nicola blinked. A second ago this man's face had seemed like something from a horror movie. Now he suddenly looked like a kind bus driver.

"You want to sign the petition?" she said incredulously.

"Yes! We've had it up to here!" The leader indicated the top of his forehead. "Enrico is a horrible boss. Never says thank-you. Never says please. I mean, I've got twenty years experience as a thug, I deserve a bit more respect."

Nicola fished a pen out of her backpack and handed it over. She tightened her knees around her saddle because Quicksilver was quivering suspiciously, as if he were laughing.

"Thanks." The lead thug laboriously signed his name and handed the pen to the thug behind him.

"And to be honest," he said confidentially to Nicola, "the guy has turned out to be a bit of a *wimp*. I mean, did you see him freaking out just because you threw a few little buttons at him? What was that all about?"

"I don't know," said Nicola. She was watching the petition get longer and longer as each thug unrolled a little more parchment and signed their names (they all had very large handwriting), and she could feel an enormous grin tugging at the corners of her mouth.

"Also, the wife and I used to like to disco dance," said the thug thoughtfully. "I'd forgotten about that until you played that music. It's about time we got rid of that stupid Quiet Please Decree."

"And I'm sick of being a hairity," said another thug. "Strands of my hair are always getting stuck in the bath drain. I wouldn't mind a crew cut."

The last thug signed the petition and handed the pen back to Nicola.

"Let's see how long it is now." The thug leader rubbed his meaty hands together.

Nicola took the petition and flew Quicksilver to where the rainbow ended. She crouched down and placed the end of the petition on the snowy ground in the splash of colorful light where the rainbow ended.

It was exactly the right length.

"Whooo hoooo!" Topaz went crazy at the other end of the rainbow.

"Hooray!" shouted the crowd, and once again, dizzy babies were tossed in the air and couples kissed.

As the people of Shobble continued to hoot and holler and whistle and cheer, Nicola and Topaz flew their Shob-Gobbles back toward Enrico.

He was sitting cross-legged in the snow playing with his hair and looking moody. His wife and children were stunned and silent in their sleigh.

"Enrico, I hereby present you with a petition as long as a rainbow calling for your resignation," said Topaz and handed over the pink parchment.

"I could just ignore the silly old constitution," said Enrico.

"Young man, ignoring the constitution carries a penalty of twenty years' exile on the planet of Arth." It was Horatio Banks, emerging from the crowd and looking extremely schoolteacherish.

"Mr. Banks!" Enrico's eyes darted about and he ducked his head like a schoolboy.

"I'm very disappointed in you, Enrico," said Horatio. "You had such *potential*!"

Enrico stuck his lower lip out. "Nobody could make *me* go to Arth!"

"*We* could, sir," said the lead thug, appearing next to Horatio and crossing his arms across his barrel chest.

Enrico sighed theatrically. "This is very hurtful!"

"You'll get over it," said Nicola.

"Do you or do you not resign?" said Topaz.

"Oh, *whatever*, YES!" said Enrico. "You and your stupid friends win! Satisfied?"

"Very," said Nicola and Topaz together.

40

T WAS A PARTY LIKE NO OTHER. THE PEOPLE OF Shobble had been waiting years for this moment and they were determined to celebrate.

Dusty guitars, saxophones, trumpets, cellos, flutes, and violins that had been hidden in attics since the introduction of the Quiet Please Decree reappeared. People sang lustily at the top of their voices while flinging themselves about a makeshift dance floor.

Hundreds of hairities handed around a pair of scissors and gave themselves the "Katie Hobbs haircut."

Long tables with white tablecloths were set up in the snow and laid with exquisite and not-so-exquisite food. There were chocolate cakes, chocolate mousse, chocolate cookies, and chocolate pastries. There were also strange bubbling broths, odd-looking stews, and evil-smelling pies.

Nicola and the Space Brigade were treated like royalty. People brought them food and drinks, and offered to rub their feet.

"You saved our planet!" they said. "How can we ever repay you?"

"Oh, we don't need anything," said Nicola, and then she caught sight of Silent Fred watching the band playing. His face looked desperately sad and she remembered Joy telling them about his band, the Fleas.

"Can anyone help give Silent Fred his voice back?" she asked.

The call went out through the crowd and minutes later Barb Banks came running, the siren around her forehead wailing. She pulled out a large bottle labeled TONGUE BURN TONIC.

"You'll need the whole bottle," she said. Silent Fred drank it, while Joy looked on anxiously. He smacked his lips and handed the bottle back to Barb.

Everyone waited to see if it would work.

Silent Fred opened his mouth. No sound came out.

He tried again.

"Thank you," he whispered.

He cleared his throat.

"Thank *you*!" he squeaked.

He coughed.

"THANK YOU!" It was a lovely, rich, deep voice. Everyone applauded.

Silent Fred threw his top hat in the air and shouted, "I *love* my wife! I've been wanting to say that out loud for so long!" Joy joyfully wiped away tears.

"Now where are the fellas?" said Silent Fred. "It's time we got the band back together!"

Next thing he had disappeared with a group of gray-haired men and soon they were belting out the words to their old hit "Rock around the Choc" while Joy was left with instructions to bring them plenty of hot chocolate in between songs. "Mmmm," said Joy thoughtfully.

She caught sight of Tyler and said, "Oh! When I was cleaning Enrico's room, I found this under his bed."

"Yes!" said Tyler excitedly as Joy handed over the silver mini easy-ride spaceship briefcase. "I thought I might never see it again."

There was some sort of a commotion behind them and they all turned around to see Enrico ducking behind his ShobGobble while his wife, Carmelita, threw badly formed snowballs at him, yelling, *"How did you let this happen? Now you're a nobody! I'm far too beautiful to be married to a nobody!"*

The twins were still in the sleigh, looking longingly at the party and wailing. "Why is everybody talking to those stupid Earthlings?" whined Josie.

"Why aren't *we* the guests of honor at that lovely party?" whined Joseph.

"What a charming family," said Shimlara.

"Poor old Enrico," said Katie.

"Don't worry," said Serena. "I'm going to send him a very polite thank-you card, just like the constitution says. It will be my pleasure."

"Who is going to run the planet now?" asked Sean.

"There will have to be an election," said Topaz. "I'll be running for president. Joshua and Serena will be my campaign managers."

"I wish we could stay to help with the campaign," said Nicola sadly.

"Why can't you all emigrate to Shobble?" said Joshua. He gave Sean a friendly punch. "You've gotten pretty good at Head Crunch, dude."

Sean punched him back. "And you've gotten pretty good at karate."

"Can't you guys hang around for just a few more days?" pleaded Serena.

"We don't know how much time has passed on Earth," said Nicola. "Our families might be worried. We should leave now."

Greta said, "Yes, and I've got homework to do."

They all stared at her.

"What?" said Greta defensively. "I do! You probably do, too!"

"I wish we could take our ShobGobbles back to Earth with us," said Katie.

That gave Nicola a start. She realized she'd been vaguely imagining that Quicksilver would always be with her. How wonderful to ride him to school each day! But, of course, there was no room for ShobGobbles in their spaceship, and there was no such thing as indigo berries on Earth.

"We'd better go say goodbye to them," said Nicola bravely.

She found Quicksilver taking a well-deserved snooze under the shelter of a tree. "I have to go now," she whispered. Quicksilver sleepily opened his eyes and gently nuzzled her neck.

"Thank you for saving me from the river," said Nicola. Quicksilver chirped softly, his liquid brown eyes filled with sadness and wisdom.

Nicola brushed away tears. "I'll never forget you! I'll come back and visit one day, promise!" Then she turned and ran, without looking back. Even Sean had suspiciously red eyes when they all returned from saying goodbye to their ShobGobbles.

A crowd of well-wishers gathered around as Tyler set up the spaceship.

"We've got something for you," announced Topaz. (She was already wearing a badge that said VOTE 4 TOPAZ!) "It's a gift from the people of Shobble."

Four security thugs lugged over an enormous jewel-encrusted treasure chest and placed it in the spaceship's storage compartment.

Topaz lifted the treasure chest's lid so they could see its contents. "It's not the one Enrico offered you, but it's pretty good."

"There's a lifetime supply of ShobbleChoc," said Serena.

"And some leftover cold hizza from last night," said Joshua. "Tastes even better the next day."

"And just a few spare weapons we thought might come in handy for the Space Brigade's next mission," said the thug leader. "Like Micro Mirth Missiles—they make your enemies double up laughing. Surprisingly effective. Oh dear, I'm getting all emotional." The thug flapped his hands around in front of his eyes and sniffed noisily.

Horatio Banks shuffled over, together with his wife Bertha, and pointed at a small jar tucked away in the corner of the chest. "I've given each of you a limited edition gold button. They have some unusual functions you might appreciate one day." He shook each of their hands.

"Katie! Oh, Katie! We'll dedicate the rest of our lives to keeping your memory alive!" The Katie Hobbs Fan Club threw themselves facedown in the snow at Katie's feet.

"Oh, for heaven's sake," sighed Katie.

"I think it's time we got out of here," said Nicola.

There were handshakes and hugs, slaps on the back, tears, and jokes as each member of the Space Brigade said their goodbyes and climbed into the spaceship.

Finally it was just Nicola left standing.

She gave Topaz a hug and said, "It's been an honor to know you, Topaz Silverbell."

"Likewise, Nicola Berry." Topaz's voice cracked and she said, "Oh, I *hate* goodbyes."

"We could never have done it without you!" Serena threw her arms around Nicola.

Joshua went to shake Nicola's hand, changed his mind, and hugged her instead. He said, "You're the nicest evil Earthling I've ever met."

Nicola couldn't speak. She smiled through her tears and before she could embarrass herself even more, she turned and climbed quickly into the spaceship.

Quietly, the Space Brigade strapped themselves into their passenger-pods.

Tyler said, "Prepare for takeoff." He punched the red button and the spaceship shot up into Shobble's atmosphere.

Nicola looked down through the arches of the rainbows and saw that the people of Shobble had organized themselves into lines and formed the words *thank you!* in huge letters across the snow.

Nicola glanced at the rest of the Space Brigade. They all had their mouths full of chocolate and blissful expressions on their faces.

"No trouble, Shobble," said Nicola softly as she turned back for one last look at the tiny glittering planet. "No trouble at all."

THE END

P.S. A Couple of Last Things That Might Interest You . . .

ICOLA STOOD UNDER A GUM TREE IN HER great-grandmother's backyard and looked up at the stars. The sounds of Grammy's 100th birthday party drifted out from the house. Nicola and Sean had given her a giant gift box of ShobbleChoc and an album of Silent Fred's hit song "Rock around the Choc." It had proved to be the most successful present of the evening. Grammy had the box of chocolates held tightly on her lap. She was refusing to share her chocolates with anyone and was nodding her head along in time to the music.

As Nicola looked up at the Milky Way, she wondered what her intergalactic friends were doing right now. Was Topaz busy handing out leaflets and giving speeches, trying to convince the people of Shobble to vote for her? Was Shimlara sunbathing under Globagaskar's two cherry suns and swimming in her fizzy pink pool with Georgio, Mully, and Squid?

She wondered also about the Space Brigade's next mission. Would there *be* another mission? It might be nice to have a little rest for a while, without any fighting off deadly Biters or hot-air ballooning in hurricanes.

Fortunately, when they'd gotten back to Earth they'd found that only three hours had passed because they'd traveled on Time Squeeze. It felt like they'd been gone for months.

Yes, it would be good not to deal with anything scarier than Mrs. Zucchini's math tests for the time being.

"Nic! They're cutting the cake!" It was Sean calling from the house.

Nicola gave the stars a secret wave and went running back into the house.

"Mum? Dad? Squid?"

Shimlara walked around her deserted house for the tenth time.

The Space Brigade had dropped her off on Globagaskar ages ago and she was still waiting for her family to come home from wherever they were. She was starting to feel a bit sad. She didn't really like being on her own and she was looking forward to telling her parents about everything that had happened.

It wasn't like them to be gone for so long without calling.

Had something bad happened? Something really bad? Shimlara kneaded her stomach. The silence in the house seemed to roar in her ears. She was going to be very cranky with her family when they returned. She was too *young* to feel worried like this. Worry was something that old people did.

She looked out the window at the swimming pool. The floating table was bobbing about, set with two mugs and a plate.

That was strange. Her parents never left dishes floating about in the swimming pool. She walked out the back to take a closer look. The mugs on the tray were full of blue-berry tea. The plate had two cookies on it. One of them had a single bite taken out of it.

Shimlara turned away from the pool and looked around the backyard. There was something lying in her little brother's sandpit. Shimlara's hand went to her mouth. It was Squid's blue security blanket. He never went *anywhere* without his blanket. She ran over, grabbed it, and hugged it tightly to her chest.

Then her eyes were caught by something else. There was a piece of torn notepaper lying on the ground next to the sandpit. She recognized her father's big loopy hand-writing. She picked it up. It said:

Help, Shiml

The last letter was wobbly as if he'd been interrupted.

As Shimlara ran back inside the house, there was just one thought in her mind.

I need the Space Brigade.

LIANE MORIARTY

had her first story published when she was ten years old. Her mother still thinks it's the best thing she's ever written. Since then she's written seven novels for adults set in the real world and three books for children set in outer space. Some of her books have been number-one best sellers and one has even been made into a TV series.

When she is not writing, she's either eating chocolate, reading in the bathtub, or standing on the side of the soccer field yelling out helpful advice to her children, even though she actually has no idea how to play.